THE TEMPERING   ATA

A John D. S. and Aida C. Truxall Book

THE

TEMPERING

GLORIA SKURZYNSKI

Afterword by
Margaret Mary Kimmel

GOLDEN TRIANGLE BOOKS

UNIVERSITY OF PITTSBURGH PRESS

Published 2000 by the University of Pittsburgh Press, Pittsburgh, Pa. 15261
Originally published by Clarion Books, Ticknor & Fields, a Houghton Mifflin Company

CONTENTS

THE TEMPERING

CHAPTER ONE

◆◆◆◆◆◆◆◆◆◆◆

FIRING

1

At a quarter past six, Karl Kerner walked the short distance down Pine Alley to the top of Center Street, whistling "Yankee Doodle Boy," a song that had been in his head since he woke up. The sky was smoky in the gray dawn. Orange flame from the blast furnaces at the bottom of Center Street glowed on each paving brick. Normally the hill would have been filled with men streaming to the mill's day shift, but only blast furnace men were supposed to report on the Fourth of July, and they'd begun work at six.

Center Street's steepness was indented by four dips—level places where teamsters could rest their horses on the long climb up—which made the hill look like a tilted five-tier cake. In the pale light, Karl noticed a figure on the dip beneath him. Even from the back, there could be no mistaking the brawny body, the snappy walk.

Breaking into a run, swinging his new dinner pail so Jame could see it, Karl yelled, "Hey, Jame! Wait up." Before he got to the dip where Jame Culley had turned to wait for him, Karl shouted, "I'm starting work in the mill today."

"Yeah? Which mill?"

"Firth Sterling—eight-inch rolling mill."

"Hey, that's the same place I work at," Jame said.

"I know. That's how I got the job, because I remembered about you. First I tried the Canaan Works employment office, but they wanted to see a birth certificate, and I won't be sixteen till November twentieth." Karl had reached Jame, and was talking fast in his eagerness to impress him. "So then I thought how you sneaked into a man's job before you were sixteen, and I tried Firth Sterling. They didn't say anything about a birth certificate, just told me to report today."

"That's swell," Jame said. "Anyway, you look sixteen. You're darn near six feet tall. Keep growing for a couple years, and you'll be as big as me . . . if you put on about fifty pounds." Jame grinned and punched Karl's arm with his big fist.

Same old Jame, Karl thought, rubbing his arm. Same, Jame—those two words rhyme. I could make up a song with them.

"So you're not going back to school, then?" Jame asked as they started down the hill together.

"Nope. What's the point of going to school, now that I have a man's job." The words filled Karl with pride and excitement all over again. He was going to be a workingman. Not a schoolboy any longer. Of course, he could have quit school at fourteen, if his parents had let him, to take one of the safer "boy" jobs in the mill. But those jobs paid hardly anything. His best friend Andy Stulak had a "boy" job, and earned only five dollars for a seven-day week. The "man" jobs paid better, but because they were more dangerous, they were forbidden to anyone under sixteen.

Jame remarked, "You sure picked a dumb day to start in the mill. Two holidays a year we're supposed to get off, Christmas and today, the Fourth of July. But Firth Sterling's got a big backlog of orders in the eight-inch mill, so that rotten foreman Baldy Weitz is making us work. I could have used a day off real bad."

"I was supposed to go on a picnic today," Karl told him, "just me and Andy Stulak. We were going to take a lunch to Kennywood Park."

"You hang around a lot with that hunky, don't you?"

Karl's step faltered out of rhythm. Andy hated to be called a hunky. Every Pole, Lithuanian, Czech, Slovak, and Hungarian in the Monongahela Valley hated the name, but every Irishman, Britisher, Scot, and German called the Central-European immigrants hunkies. If anyone else had said it, Karl would have told him off, but he knew Jame hadn't used the word in malice. Jame was big, brash, and sometimes wild, but he was too sure of himself to need to demean anyone.

The way Jame's big teeth gleamed from his bold grin, the way he wore his cap on the back of his head, tilted sideways, the way he rolled up his sleeves to show his muscular arms, all showed that Jame knew what a prime physical specimen he was. The Culleys, the Kerners, and the Stulaks lived side by side in houses fronting Chestnut Street, with Pine Alley at the back. Ever since Karl had been old enough to notice the people in the neighborhood, he'd admired Jame Culley as an ideal of manliness, even though Jame was only three years older than Karl.

They'd reached Canaan Avenue, which paralleled the Canaan Works of the Carnegie Steel Company. Usually the mill screeched and roared as it gave birth to a million tons of steel a year. On an ordinary workday, Karl and Jame would have had to shout to be heard above the clamor, but because of the holiday the mill was as close to silent as it ever became. Karl and Jame were not going to work on the west side of the Monongahela River, where the Canaan works spread out, with the town of Canaan rising on the hills behind it. They would cross the bridge to the small, independent Firth Sterling plant on the east side of the river.

"How much you going to get paid?" Jame asked.

"Ten cents an hour." It wasn't much to start with, but Karl was sure he'd get a raise pretty quickly, as soon as they saw what a good worker he'd be.

"Huh! I still only get two bucks and a half for an eleven-hour day turn, and the same for a thirteen-hour night turn," Jame said. "And I been working as a rougher for the past two years. Then they have the gall to charge two cents toll to walk across the bridge. But I never pay it."

"You don't? How do you get out of paying it?" Karl asked.

"On account of I don't walk *across* the bridge, I cross *underneath* the bridge," Jame said. "I'll show you how."

That must be one of Jame's jokes, Karl thought. "You're kidding me, huh, Jame? You trying to tell me you walk across the river?"

Jame threw back his head and laughed, his Adam's apple bobbing in his thick neck. "Don't be nutty, Karl. Walking on water's the one thing I haven't figured out how to do yet. When I said under the bridge, I meant the underside structure. On the support beams. You can shinny down beneath the bridge and walk across the main support beam, then climb up when you get to the other side. I'll show you. It'll save you four cents a day."

So Jame wasn't joking. Karl felt a chill pinch his stomach. "But I already have the four cents, Jame. My mom gave it to me."

"So, why waste the money? Hey, it ain't that scary. Nothing to it, once you get used to it."

Karl wanted to holler that he'd rather pay the toll, that the Monongahela River was close to a quarter of a mile wide and God-only-knew how deep, but he didn't want to sound like a pantywaist in front of Jame. His steps slowed as they came close to the bridge.

"Jame," he said, "won't we need both hands to hang on? How can we cross underneath the bridge if we're carrying dinner pails?"

"Easy. Just unbuckle your belt, stick the belt through the handle of the pail, and buckle it up again. Only buckle it tight, so your pants won't fall down. You wouldn't want your pants hanging down around your knees when you're fifty feet above the river."

Prickles of fear danced across Karl's scalp. Mentally whispering, "God have mercy on me," he slipped his belt through the dinner pail's handle, rebuckling it on the tightest hole. Then he swung over the bridge railing, as Jame had done, and climbed down a pillar to the big main support beam that ran parallel beneath the bridge.

He was still above dry land. Below him, railroad tracks sliced clean and shining through the grime of fallen bits of coal. Feeling like a tightrope walker, even though the beam he stood on was a foot wide, Karl turned to face the river.

Jame was already twenty feet ahead of him on the support beam, balancing as casually as if he were strolling along a boardwalk.

Karl's fingers clamped around the triangular trusses that stretched from the beam to the bridge roadbed overhead. Taking a deep breath, he moved his feet forward on the steel beam. It felt firm and solid. Confidence seeped into him and he walked faster, until he made the mistake of looking down.

The quiet waters of the Monongahela swept beneath him, wide, deep, and awesome, reflecting the pearl of morning sky around rippled images of blast-furnace flame. The river seemed so far *down*, much farther down than when Karl had crossed the bridge the way people were supposed to, on the part made for people to walk on and streetcars to ride on and horses to pull wagons across. What kind of crazy thing was he doing?— hanging onto the underside of a bridge!

Quickly, he looked up to erase the specter of the river, but the damage was done. His anklebones felt as though they'd dissolved.

He could move each rubbery foot no more than an inch at a time. When he reached for the next handhold, his sweat-soaked palms slipped off the steel truss. Panicked, he flailed both arms in a grab for the truss and clung to it, unable to move at all.

Jame was leaning against the first piling that supported the bridge, arms folded across his chest—not even holding on! With terror-filled eyes, Karl implored for help.

"How's your sister Kathleen?" Jame asked him.

"She's f . . . fine," Karl answered, his voice shaking.

"What's she doing these days?" Jame asked.

"She plays piano at the nickelodeon movie theater, six nights a week." It was ridiculous! Karl was frozen with fear, certain he was going to fall into the river and drown before he ever got a chance to be a steelworker, and Jame kept asking him silly questions, as though they were having a chat on the back porch.

"Will Kathleen be going back to school?" Jame asked, turning his back on Karl and beginning to cross the girder to the next piling.

"Yep. She'll be in eleventh grade this year." Karl had to strain to manage a sensible answer, but the effort of concentrating on his speech kept him from looking at the river. He was able to move his foot, to take a step. "Mom says that since Kathleen earns three dollars a week just working evenings, she should stay in school. And Kathleen wants to stay." Karl took another step.

From ahead, Jame called back, "Now you should ask me how my sister Mary Margaret is."

"Why should I ask that?" Karl said through clenched jaws.

"Because Mary Margaret's sweet on you."

Karl bit his lip and slid his hands forward on the steel truss. Jame's comment about Mary Margaret caught him so off-guard that his muscles loosened enough for him to move forward. If Mary Margaret weren't Jame's sister, and if Karl hadn't been so concerned about clinging for his life to the underside of a bridge, he'd have shot back a nasty insult.

Short, bow-legged Mayo Culley and his four-foot-ten-inch wife, Bridey, were Jame's unlikely parents. In one heroic burst of creation they had produced the mighty Jame, but afterward they never came close to making another like him. The younger Culley children—Mary Margaret, Francis X, and the three little Marys—carried their slight resemblance to Jame on skinny bodies.

Mary Margaret, the same age as Karl, was shy to the point of wordlessness, and held her thin shoulders stooped as if to cringe from the world. The facial features that made Jame handsome were slightly off-balance in Mary Margaret, enough to deny her any obvious prettiness. It was no good news to Karl that Mary Margaret was sweet on him, but it distracted him from his terror of falling.

Never looking back, Jame continued to ask trivial questions, and Karl kept answering them, until they'd crossed to the east riverbank and climbed the last steel pillar to the surface. Only when they stood once more on firm, solid roadway did Karl's heart slow its frantic hammering. He breathed deeply in the smoky air, wildly relieved that he wasn't fighting for breath beneath the surface of the Monongahela River.

"There, see? Two pennies saved is two pennies earned, huh, Karl?" Jame squeezed Karl's arm. "You were kinda scared back there, but you did real good for the first time."

"First time!" Karl exclaimed. "There isn't going to be any other time, Jame, not for me. Listen, when we go home tonight, we'll both walk on top of the bridge, all right? My treat."

"Sure." Jame laughed as he removed the dinner-pail handle from his belt. "After eleven hours in the rolling mill, you'll be too tired to hang like a monkey, anyhow. Let's get going before the whistle blows."

After a five-minute diagonal trot toward the riverbank, they reached the rolling mill, a large building constructed of sheet metal. Karl hung back, suddenly taken with a fresh set of jitters.

"What's wrong?" Jame asked.

"It's ... kinda big." What if he couldn't find his way around the inside? Maybe he'd get lost and they'd fire him, and he'd have to go back to being a schoolboy.

"That ain't just the eight-inch mill in there," Jame said. "The ten-inch mill's in there, too, and the roll storage places and stuff like that. You never been inside it?"

"No. I just went to the employment office."

"Come on, then. I'll take you to the foreman so you can find out what you're supposed to do. But first, listen, I got to warn you about him," Jame said. "Baldy Weitz is a rotten bugger. Watch him close, Karl, and if he tells you to jump, jump fast. If you don't, he'll throw you out on your can faster than you can spit."

Karl still hadn't calmed down from the bridge scare; Jame's warning made his insides twist even more. The mill building seemed grim and threatening. No windows broke the expanse of walls. The interior of the building was illuminated by electric lights high overhead. Karl followed Jame along the metal floor toward a thin, bald-headed man who was squinting at the pages of an order form.

"Mr. Weitz," Jame said, "this is Karl Kerner. He was hired on to start today. What job do you want him to do?"

Karl smiled brightly, trying to look smart and alert, but the foreman's cold blue eyes drifted disinterestedly over him. "Start him as a smoke-hole boy," Weitz told Jame. "You show him ..." The words were interrupted by the blast of the seven-o'clock whistle. " ... the ropes," Weitz continued when the piercing whistle died. "And get a move on it, Culley. I want to begin the first heat fast. It'll be number 297."

"Smoke-hole boy—that's the same job I started on," Jame

said as he led Karl to a storage area. "Now see, these things are billets." He pointed to a pile of steel bars scattered in a disorderly heap. "This first heat's going to be an easy one for you to get broke in on. A baby could do it. Just pick up the two-foot billets with number 297 chalked on them. Load them onto this handcart, five or six at a time, if you're strong enough to push that many. Then truck them over to the smoke hole."

"Where's the smoke hole?" Karl asked, looking around, half expecting to see a hole in the floor with smoke coming out of it.

"It's the warming end of the big heating furnace over there. Just unload the billets next to that red-headed Irishman—he's Big John Reilly, and he's the heater. He puts the billets into the smoke hole first, then into the furnace. So all you got to do is take the right billets over to Big John. Got it?"

"Yep, I think so," Karl answered, although his anxiety had made Jame's simple directions sound complicated.

"Then get started. The furnace is firing up already—we'll be rolling in about forty minutes. Remember, if Baldy Weitz starts eyeing you, jump around like you're working your hind end off."

After Jame left, Karl picked up the first billet. He expected it to be heavier than it was, but the two-by-two-inch, two-foot billet weighed only about thirty pounds. He loaded six of them onto the handcart, struggled to push it, then unloaded one billet and trundled the rest across the floor to the furnace, skidding as he pulled to a stop.

The red-headed Irishman was hunkered down, relaxing with the stem of a corn-cob pipe clamped in his teeth. "Hello, kid," Big John said. "What's your moniker?"

"My name's Karl, Mr. Reilly." With his shirtsleeve, Karl wiped the sweat from his upper lip.

"You can call me Big John, but if you don't get them billets over here fast enough, I'll call you all kinds of nasty names in Gaelic that you won't understand." Big John raised himself to a stand, clearing well over six feet. "Ah, just jokin' you, kid," he said. "Me, I ain't so fierce. Baldy Weitz is the mug you got to run your stumps off for."

Karl raced back to the billet pile, certain that Baldy Weitz's eyes must be boring into his back, although he wasn't even sure where the foreman was standing. In the half hour before the first rolling began, Karl made six trips to transfer billets to Big John Reilly. After he'd finished unloading the sixth batch, Big John said to him, "Stick around for a minute, kid. Baldy Weitz ain't here–he's gone up to the shipping department for a while. We're right now ready to roll, so if you hang around, you'll get a chance to see your friend Culley doin' some fancy footwork."

While he was speaking, Big John had put on heavy work gloves, then picked up a pair of yard-long tongs. Throwing open the furnace door, he yelled, "Start the rolls!"

Big John was wearing a flannel shirt from which the sleeves had been cut at the shoulders; the glow from the furnace gilded his thick biceps. With the tongs, he reached inside the furnace to clamp one end of a red-hot billet. Karl leaped back from the shower of sparks as Big John flung down the billet so it slid across the steel floor to Jame.

Jame picked up the glowing billet with his own tongs, and jammed one end of it against a groove in a pair of rolls that looked like the wringer on Karl's mother's washing machine. With a scream of steel against steel, the roll bit the red-hot billet and forced it along a groove narrower than the billet's thickness. When it came out the other side of the roll, the billet was oval-shaped and a foot longer than it had been on the way in. The instant the billet cleared the roll, Jame picked up another one, fresh from the furnace, and started that one through.

A fat man with the longest handlebar mustache Karl had ever seen caught the first billet with tongs and passed it back over the top of the roll to Jame, who rammed it into an adjoining roll. Immediately Jame bent to pick up still another billet from the floor.

So much was happening so fast that Karl had trouble following it all. His senses were jolted by the blinding glare from superheated billets, by the scorching spray of sparks as Big John flung the billets across the floor with such force that they came to a stop only inches from Jame's feet, by the harsh shriek of steel being devoured by rolls. With each pass down the row of rolls, each billet became narrower and longer, until it snaked out of the sixth and final roll as a fiery round rod half an inch in diameter and thirty feet long.

Bending, twisting, thrusting, Jame was in constant motion. His work shirt darkened with perspiration under the arms and in spreading patches of dampness both front and back. Karl was filled with admiration for Jame, and with hope that before too long, he could be promoted to a job like Jame's.

"That Culley's the best rougher I ever seen," Big John bawled to Karl. The man shouted to be heard above the grating noise of the steel, never missing a beat as he pulled billets out of the furnace. "But that's enough gawkin' for now, boy. I'm runnin' out of billets for the smoke hole, so get along and bring me some more."

2

After four hours spent hauling steel, Karl's shoulders burned with fatigue. Lifting one thirty-pound billet might be a baby's game, but a hundred in a row were enough to make any grown man long for a break. He'd already moved a ton and a half of steel, and it wasn't yet noon. Then, to his surprise, he couldn't find any more billets chalk-marked 297. With relief, he realized that his work was finished until loading for the next heat began.

All that time Jame had been bouncing back and forth at the rolls like a street-corner dancer diving for pennies. He seemed to do twice as much work as the other four men along the rolls. No, Karl thought, Jame must have worked ten times harder than the fat man with the handlebar mustache, across from Jame, whose only job was to return billets across the first roll.

While Karl stood wondering whether he dared leave the loading area to get a drink of water, the foreman, Baldy Weitz, shouted, "That's the end of number 297. Shut 'er down now till we get the next order ready." With a squeal and clatter that died to a moan and then sweet quiet, the rolls stopped.

Karl watched Jame run to the water bucket and lift it head high, gulping such big swallows his throat swelled. Then Jame walked over to Karl and said, "Better grab your grub before the next heat starts. You can eat fast while you're waiting for Weitz to tell you which billets get loaded next. Come on, I'll eat with you."

"I don't know how you can do all that work, Jame," Karl said when they were sitting on a bench with their dinner pails between them. "Don't you get tired?" Karl was almost too tired to eat, but he swallowed his first sandwich half-chewed, expecting Baldy Weitz to yell for him any minute.

Jame laughed. "That was an easy order. You ought to see when we handle the four-by-four-inch billets that are six feet long. They're the ones that bulge your muscles. But you won't have to lug any of them big buggers today. The next order coming up's a short one—we'll finish it in a couple of hours."

Karl commented, "That fat guy across from you doesn't look like he works any too hard."

"Oh, him." Jame spat on the floor. "That's Dutch Schwenk. He's got no business on this job, someone as old as him. Rolling mill work is a young man's job. You got to be strong and quick on your feet, or else you bollix up the whole works. Schwenk's a fat, lazy slug. But he's some kind of relative to Baldy Weitz, so Weitz keeps him on."

Jame shoved a whole hard-boiled egg into his mouth as Karl finished the third of his ham sandwiches and started on his pie. While he chewed, Jame said, "Look at Dutch, settin' over there playing with his mustache. He thinks that mustache is as classy as Lady Astor's pet horse." Jame chuckled to himself.

Leaning back against a post, Dutch Schwenk had his eyes closed. The thumbs and forefingers of both his hands slid along the length of his mustache, again and again, beginning under his nose and ending beyond his cheeks, where they curled the ends of the handlebars.

"That mustache must be eight inches long on each side,"

Karl remarked. When Schwenk let go, the handlebars stood out as though they'd been starched.

"And is he crazy about it!" Jame said. "Every time we get a rest, Dutch plays lovey-dovey with that mustache." Jame laughed silently, his thick shoulders shaking. Since it wasn't like Jame to laugh without making a lot of noise, Karl looked at him in surprise.

"What's so funny?" he asked.

"Just anticipatin'," Jame said, with a grin.

"Anticipating what?"

Jame wiped his mouth with his wrist and leaned toward Karl. Amusement glittered in his eyes. "You're my pal, Karl, so I'll let you in on something. Today's the Fourth of July, right? We got to work, right? But it seems to me we should have a little fun, a little fireworks on the holiday. I won't tell you just what's gonna happen, but after the next heat's over, we'll have a long break before the one after that. If I know Dutch Schwenk, he'll fall asleep for a while. That's when I want you to keep your eyes peeled good and hard."

"What are you going to do, Jame?" Karl asked, a laugh already rising in his chest. When Jame was in a mood to act the clown, he could make a wooden Indian fall down laughing. At the same time Karl felt uneasy, because when Jame got too high-spirited, he could really raise the roof, shingle by shingle.

"What am I gonna do? That's for me to know and you to find out," Jame answered, dropping one eyelid in a sly wink.

"Smoke-hole boy!" Baldy Weitz yelled. "Get over here and start loading number 431."

Karl jumped up quickly to show the foreman how eager

he was to get back to work, but Jame grabbed his arm. "Look at that, your hands are blistering," Jame said.

"A little bit, maybe."

"You need work gloves. They don't give 'em to us, you have to buy your own. I got an extra pair—wait a minute, I'll go get 'em. They're an old pair, with holes where they were burned through from sparks, but they'll keep the billets from rubbing any more blisters on you."

Jame's gloves were too big for Karl, but he wore them anyway, flattered that Jame was concerned for him. The billets for the second heat were again two inches square, but at three feet in length they were half again as heavy as the first ones. Karl could manage to push only three at a time on the handcart. Luckily, the order was for just five dozen rods, and it was filled more quickly than the first one had been. By the time he'd loaded the last of the billets chalk-marked 431, Karl was glad to drop on the bench and rest.

After the rolls had shut down, Jame sat beside him, looking as fresh and lively as he had when the seven o'clock whistle blew, although his shirt was so soaked with perspiration that not a dry inch showed. Jame smelled pretty ripe after all his exertion, but Karl realized that he didn't smell like any lily himself.

"Watch Dutch Schwenk now," Jame whispered, "and see how fast he falls asleep. Give him two minutes; he'll be snoring like he's sawing logs."

Jame reached under the bench for his dinner pail, lifted it up and set it beside him. He raised the lid, feeling inside to pull out the bottom compartment cover—the enameled dinner pail had three tiers, the lowest one made to hold coffee.

Jame's big fist came over the top of the pail holding a pair of scissors.

Karl's eyes widened. "Jame, what are you up to?"

"Is Dutch Schwenk asleep?"

"Looks like it. He's snoring."

Jame stood up and aimed a wink at the other men on the crew, who'd gathered in a tight knot, their faces nearly split with grins. Then Jame tiptoed, as much as a man his size could tiptoe, to the bench where Dutch Schwenk dozed. Holding the scissors as carefully as a surgeon, Jame leaned forward and snipped. One side of Schwenk's long mustache fell to the floor, looking like an amputated cat's tail.

Karl's breath caught in his throat, blocking a giggle that wanted to escape. Big John Reilly and the three catchers got red in the face trying to keep from laughing out loud; they were afraid they'd alert Baldy Weitz, who was inspecting the last order of rods. The harder they tried to keep quiet, though, the more the men sputtered and snorted. Baldy Weitz's head shot up, but Jame had already gone back to the bench to sit innocently beside Karl, and the scissors were back in the dinner pail.

"What the hell's goin' on?" Baldy Weitz barked, making Dutch Schwenk stir in his sleep. In a dreamlike motion, Schwenk's hands moved up to stroke his mustache. The left hand found the usual long handlebar, but the right hand fumbled, then frantically patted the bare half of his face as his eyes flew open.

"*Gott in Himmel!*" Schwenk bellowed. The crewmen exploded with laughter, all except Karl, who was frightened over what was happening, and Jame, who kept a virtuous expression.

Dutch Schwenk's face turned purple as his wild eyes turned on Jame. "You . . . you!" he roared, and Jame answered, "Who, me? You want me, Dutch?"

Schwenk's fury exploded into action. He rushed to the billet storage area to grab a three-foot billet, but Jame had turned to enjoy the laughs from his fellow workers, so he didn't see Schwenk run toward him holding the billet like a baseball bat.

"Jame! Duck!" Karl screamed, throwing himself out of the way of the maddened Schwenk. Instinct made Jame dive forward, but not far enough. The billet glanced off the crown of his head, and his big body crumpled to the floor.

"Jame!" Karl cried, kneeling over him while the crewmen wrestled to take the billet away from Schwenk. Jame's face was white as death; his forehead felt damp and cold.

"He's bleeding," Karl shouted to Big John Reilly. "His head's cut."

Big John picked up a full bucket and dumped cold water in a rush over Jame's head. Jame groaned and tried to sit up, but fell backward again.

"Just let the dumb bugger lay there," Baldy Weitz yelled. "He got what he was asking for, the son of a . . . " Instead of concerning himself with Jame's bleeding head, Weitz picked up the billet and carried it back to the storage area, where he flung it in disgust on top of the pile.

On the other bench, Dutch Schwenk sat slumped, tears running down his cheeks. "Six years it took me to grow it this long," he moaned. "Six whole years shot to hell." If Karl hadn't been so worried about Jame, he might have felt sorry for Dutch Schwenk, who looked ridiculous with half a mustache.

"All you hooligans get yourselves back and start the next

heat," Baldy Weitz bawled. "Clyde, you be the rougher from now on. We'll have to work shorthanded for the rest of the day. Albert, go over to the ten-inch mill and see if they can spare us a smoke-hole boy. You . . . !" Weitz stabbed his finger at Karl. "Get that jackass Culley out of here. Take him home. He's finished in this mill."

"How can I take him home?" Karl pleaded. "He can't even stand."

Weitz sneered, "He'll be able to stand. A crack on the head won't hurt the likes of him. He's got pickled pigs' feet where his brains oughta be."

Karl pulled Jame's arms to try to lift him, but Jame's head rolled backward on his limp body.

"Pick him up and carry him," Weitz ordered. "Throw him over your shoulders."

"He weighs two hundred pounds!"

Weitz's eyes narrowed as though he were examining Karl for the first time that day. "How old are you?" he asked.

"Sixteen."

"What's your birth date?"

"November twentieth, eighteen ninety–f . . . five," Karl stammered.

Weitz's lip curled. "When you come back tomorrow, bring your birth certificate. Now get that thick mick out of here. And when he can hear again, tell him he's fired too."

"Jame's not a mick," Karl muttered. "He was born in America." Then Weitz's words struck him. "Fired . . . too? You mean I'm fired?"

"Why, no." Weitz didn't bother to hide the sarcasm in his voice. "You'll have your job back whenever you bring the birth certificate that proves you're sixteen." He turned and stomped off, yelling, "Come on, Dutch, quit your bellyaching."

Karl felt as if he'd been hit in his middle with the same billet that had felled Jame. He'd lost his job! After less than a day, he'd lost it. And all because of Jame's foolish practical joke. He pinched Jame hard, to make him come awake, resisting the urge to punch his friend in the nose for making him lose his job.

"Move over, kid. Let me help you." Big John Reilly hauled Jame to his feet, but Jame's legs curled like wilted celery. "Stick your arm under his shoulder, Karl," Big John said. "I'll get him past the door for you, but after that you'll have to lug him home somehow on your own."

After they'd dragged unconscious Jame outside the building, Big John snapped his fingers, saying, "Wait a minute! I got a brainstorm." He leaned Jame against the sheet-steel wall of the building, telling Karl, "Keep him propped up till I get back."

Jame had opened his eyes, but they didn't focus—the green of his eyes looked glassy. He stared at Karl as though he couldn't decide who Karl was, or what the two of them were doing outside in the hot sun. As they waited, Karl struggled to keep Jame's sagging body from slipping to the ground, but his mind was on the loss of his job, not on Jame. Deep disappointment made his eyes sting, made his nose feel runny. Since he couldn't let go of Jame, Karl rubbed his nose against the sleeve of his shirt.

"Here's something that oughta work," Big John announced when he returned. "This old handcart was dumped because it's all wore out, but it'll probably hold Jame for one trip." Big John propped the handles of the cart against the wall, then lowered Jame into it. "His legs is gonna hang out and drag, but you oughta be able to pull him if you walk backwards. That's the best I can do." Big John shook his head. "I'm gonna miss that crazy Culley. Best damn rougher in the whole steel industry. When he comes into his head, tell him it was a great shenanigan he pulled. He'll want to hear that."

Clyde, the catcher who was now a rougher, had come to the door. "Big John," he said, "you better get inside mighty fast. Weitz is squawkin' like a rooster with a rupture. Here, I brought Jame's hat." Clyde gently set the peaked cap on Jame's chest. "And here's the two dinner pails. You can hang them over the cart handles."

"I'll say a Hail Mary that you make it home," Big John called back as he hurried into the mill.

"We'll need more than a Hail Mary," Karl muttered. He took the handles of the handcart and began to pull it, walking backward across the mill yard, straining under the burden of Jame's weight. Jame's head was at the top of the cart, nearest the handles; his back lay flat against the bed of the cart; his legs dangled over the edge. The heels of Jame's work shoes scraped wavy furrows that crisscrossed the wheel tracks in the grit of the mill yard.

The macadamized yard was level; when they came to the end of it, Karl tried to figure how he could ever pull all that weight up the unpaved incline to the bridge. He noticed four little black boys, the oldest about twelve, picking up bits of coal that had dropped along the railroad tracks. All of them were thin and barefoot, but they were the only persons in sight, and Karl needed help.

"Hey, you guys, come give me a hand, will you?" he called. The boys straightened, spreading hands above their eyes to see better in the bright sunlight. They dropped their burlap sack beside the track and moved toward Karl, walking in a tight bunch, giggling at the sight of Jame.

"You fellows push the bottom of the cart there, and I'll pull," Karl told them. "I've got to get up to the bridge."

The four boys pushed against the cart, laughing as though it was the funniest job they'd ever been asked to do. "How much you gonna pay us, boss?" the oldest wanted to know.

To give himself time to think, Karl pretended he was too winded to answer right away. All he had was the four pennies in his pocket, and he'd need that to pay the toll for himself and Jame. But if he didn't promise the boys something, they might stop helping him, and he could never manage to pull Jame up the incline all by himself.

"A couple of pennies," he answered, relieved when the boys kept pushing, but irritated because they wouldn't stop giggling. Karl felt rotten enough about being fired; he didn't need the extra irritant of the boys' giggles.

When they reached the toll booth, the oldest boy held out his hand, but Karl stalled him, saying, "Wait a minute. Just stand right there. I'll be back."

The toll taker wouldn't look up from the newspaper he was reading until Karl finally said, "Hey, mister, I got trouble. My pal's been hurt, and I have to take him home over the bridge, but I only have four cents."

"That's all you need, sonny," the man said. "Two cents for you and two cents for your pal."

"I know, but, see . . . I had to get some colored kids to help me bring him up from the mill, and I promised I'd pay them too."

"That's your hard luck, sonny." The toll man peered around

the edge of his newspaper at the cart; Karl had leaned it against the bridge railing. "Is that your pal? Jame Culley?"

"Yep, it's Jame all right," Karl said as the toll man began to laugh.

"The great Jame Culley gettin' drug home in a wheelbarrer," the man said. "Well, if that don't beat all! Somebody finally clobbered him over the head with a two-by-four, huh?"

"No, mister, with a three-foot steel billet," Karl replied.

Laying down his paper, the toll man said, "I figger the big chump owes me about ten dollars' worth of toll, but you know …" His whiskery face creased in a grin. "I like that wild son of a gun. Every day I watch him risk his neck under the bridge—it adds a little tingle to my life. Go on, give your pennies to them darky kids. Jame can have a free trip today. You too."

Karl let out his breath. "Thanks, mister."

"Hope his head ain't hurt too bad."

Karl paid the four boys, then strained to start the cart across the bridge. If Jame's feet hadn't been dragging, the cart could have built some momentum of its own so it wouldn't be so heavy to pull. Karl stopped after a little way and bent Jame's legs at the knees, bracing Jame's heavy work shoes against the sides of the cart. After that it was easier to pull.

Hard as it was to drag Jame across the level bridge, Karl wondered how he'd ever get him up Center Street. There was no way he could manage it alone; he'd have to find help. And what would Mayo and Bridey Culley say when Karl brought their son home, bloody and knocked senseless, and was forced to tell them that Jame had lost his job?

Karl felt terrible enough about his own lost job, but his father, Hugo Kerner, was subforeman on the open hearth, and he made good pay. Jame's father, Mayo Culley, had been out of work for five years, ever since his hand had been mangled in a mill accident. Bridey Culley took in washing to earn money, but Jame brought the only dependable income into the family. Or he had, until that day.

A surge of anger flowed through Karl toward the drooping form of Jame, who was at last showing some sign of life by raising his hand to wave away the flies that buzzed around the clotted blood in his red-gold hair. Why had Jame pulled such a dumb stunt just to get a laugh? Why had he thought he could get away with it? Of course, Schwenk and Weitz could tell that Jame had done it—Jame was the only one sitting there looking as pure as an altar boy, while the rest of the men were splitting their sides laughing.

So why hadn't Jame thought ahead, figured out that he might lose his job? Karl felt sorry for Jame, but he felt a lot sorrier for himself. He'd been so excited about getting hired for a man's job, even though he wasn't old enough. When he'd dressed in work clothes that morning and started down the hill holding his brand-new dinner pail, he'd wanted to run and holler in exhilaration, because he was going inside the mill to be a steelworker. Now he was back on the outside again, out of a job, out of the mills. And to make things even worse, since he'd lost this job, his parents would expect him to stay in school until his sixteenth birthday.

A huckster with a wagon nearly emptied of vegetables came toward them, traveling in the opposite direction across the bridge. When he got close, the huckster's mouth dropped open at the sight of Karl and Jame. He let the reins hang slack over the horse's back, twisting his head all the way around as the wagon passed, until his neck wouldn't turn any farther.

"Gettin' a good eyeful, mister?" Karl shouted angrily, but the huckster only laughed, showing gaps in his teeth.

Karl realized they must look ridiculous: He walking backward pulling the cart, glancing over his shoulder to make sure he didn't trip into any holes in the macadam; Jame, with his knees tucked under his chin, looking like a drunk being carted home after a binge; the two dinner pails swinging crazily from the cart handles. Karl felt his cheeks redden as humiliation fueled his anger. When he looked at Jame, though, his resentment softened. Jame looked too battered for Karl to stay mad at him. It was lucky Jame hadn't been killed. And to be honest, it wasn't really his fault that Karl had gotten fired— at least not directly. Jame would never have wanted to get Karl in trouble. Jame was his friend.

By the time they reached the end of the bridge and turned onto Canaan Avenue, Karl was as hot, sticky, and worn out as he'd ever felt in his life. Jame had started to mutter, but was still out of his head.

"I must of really tied one on. Baldy Weitz'll kill me if I show up drunk. They call it the eight-inch mill, Karl, because the rolls are eight inches in diameter." Twisting from side to side, Jame said, "Kathleen. Beautiful, beautiful Kathleen."

Karl's head jerked at the sound of his sister's name. Could Jame be sweet on Kathleen? If he was, and Karl's mother Maggie Rose Kerner ever found out about it, her temper would shoot off like a skyrocket. Maggie Rose already had her Irish dander up against all the Culleys.

On one of his backward glances to check his footing, Karl noticed Andy Stulak ahead of him on Canaan Avenue, coming out of Santori's Grocery. "Andy!" Karl shouted. "Over here. I need you."

Andy ran toward him, yelling, "Holy mackerel! What happened to Jame?" Andy's face was smudged with soot from the mill. His gray eyes widened as he stared at Jame, making him look like an end man in a minstrel show, only with blond hair.

Karl answered, "He had an accident. I'll tell you on the way. You'll have to help me pull him up Center Street."

"I don't think both of us together could drag him up that steep hill," Andy said, "but I can go home and get my old man and the Hrenko brothers to help. You look dead beat, Karl. Let me take this cart and pull Jame into some shade."

"Thanks." Karl gratefully surrendered the handles of the cart. His shoulders felt as though they'd been pulled out of their sockets, and he was desperately thirsty. "I'm going into Santori's Grocery and ask for a drink of water," he said. "You stay with Jame."

"Santori's," Jame moaned. "Ice."

"What's he saying?" Andy asked.

"Ice," Jame repeated. He fingered the cut on his head. "Ice. Here."

Karl said, "He's coming out of it. He wants some ice on his head. I'll go get it." Karl stumbled into the grocery and found Ector Santori standing on a ladder, wiping soot off the tops of cans.

"Mr. Santori, Jame Culley got a nasty crack on his head," Karl told him. "Can I have some ice for it?"

"Jame Culley? You betcha, Karl. Jame got hurt? How'd it happen?" Ector Santori climbed down the ladder to lean over the counter, his aproned belly bulging above the edge.

"A guy in the rolling mill hit him. Jame was knocked cold. He's just started coming around now, and he wants some ice for his head." Karl wondered whether he could ask for a drink of water, but decided he'd better get the ice first.

"Wait there. I bringa the ice." Ector Santori took an ice pick to the cooler in the back where soda pop and bottled beer were stored. He came back carrying a big chunk of ice, and said, "I go an' see Jame. I lika Jame. He makes me laugh alla time."

Outside, Ector Santori held the ice against the swollen lump on the top of Jame's head until the ice melted, smearing the blood. "He's plenty hurt," Santori said. "How you gonna get him uppa the hill?"

"I'm gonna fetch my father and the boarders," Andy answered. "They can carry him."

"No, Andy, you help me hitch the horse and bringa the wagon. We take him home in my grocery wagon. My missus can watch the store while I'm gone."

"That's a swell idea, Mr. Santori." Karl dropped to the doorstep of the grocery store, glad the responsibility for Jame was finally taken off his aching shoulders. Now maybe he could get a drink of water, before he had to climb Center Street himself and tell his parents that he was out of work. His parents wouldn't care, but Karl sure did.

3

That night Karl looked differently at Kathleen.

For fifteen years he'd thought of Kathleen only as a sister, someone who'd been part of his life since his earliest memory. He'd never paid much attention to the way she looked, except to vaguely realize that she was pretty, with dark hair, light blue eyes, and fair skin just like his own. "Black Irish" looks, their mother called them. Even though their mother,

Maggie Rose, was blond and blue-eyed, she claimed that in Ireland, her Hannon family had many relatives of close blood with Black Irish coloring. From time to time, Hugo Kerner mildly reminded Maggie Rose that his own hair was dark, that his own eyes were blue, that the German Kerners could claim as much responsibility as the Irish Hannons for the way the children looked.

On that Fourth of July evening, as all the Kerners sat on their back porch hoping for any small breeze to relieve the heat and the humidity, Karl studied Kathleen with new interest, because Jame Culley in his rambling talk had called her beautiful. Kathleen perched on the edge of the porch. The night sky, colored orange from blast furnace flame, made leaf shadows on her face and her throat, which was bared beneath the unbuttoned collar of her shirtwaist. She'd taken off her shoes and black stockings to curl her toes around the porch boards. She had nice ankles, Karl noticed.

To amuse the youngest of his three children, a five-year-old boy nicknamed Hunnie, Hugo Kerner blew train-whistle sounds on his harmonica, warming it up before he began a song. Homemade music was the chief family entertainment in Canaan, Pennsylvania, because it didn't cost anything, and because there wasn't much else to do.

From the porch swing where he sat next to his wife, Maggie Rose, Hugo told everyone, "Think of a song."

"'Always in the Way,'" Hunnie suggested promptly.

Kathleen laughed, saying, "We're not going to *start* with that one, are we? Can't we have a few happy songs before Hunnie starts to cry?"

"I won't cry," Hunnie declared.

"You always ask for 'Always in the Way' and you say you

won't cry, but you always do," Kathleen teased her little brother.

"I won't cry this time," Hunnie promised. He was sitting on his mother's lap, his blond head resting beneath her chin, his bare legs pale against the darkness of her skirt.

"How about 'I'll Take You Home Again, Kathleen'?" Maggie Rose asked, trying to sidetrack Hunnie.

"'Always in the Way,'" Hunnie insisted.

Karl sighed. "Might as well get it over with."

Hugo blew a few breaths into the mouth organ to clear it, then played the opening chord as the family eased into the usual harmony.

> Please, mister, take me in your car,
> I want to see Ma-ma,
> They say she's up in heaven,
> Is it very, very far?

The corners of Hunnie's mouth pulled down, but he scowled, determined not to cry.

> My new Ma-ma is very cross,
> She will not let me play,
> My old Ma-ma would never say . . .

Hunnie's chin trembled; his mouth stretched into weeping position.

> You're always in the way.

At the chorus, Hunnie gave up his struggle to control the tears.

> Always in the way,
> So they always say,

My old Ma-ma would never say,
I'm always in the way.

The little boy buried his face against his mother's breast and let the sobs come, but the Kerners had been through so many repetitions of the scene that, hardly pausing to catch breath, they plunged into the song always used as an anti-dote to Hunnie's sadness:

I took my girl to a fancy ball,
It was a social hop,
We danced until the lights went out,
The music it did stop,
I took her to a restaurant,
The best one on the street,
She said she wasn't hungry,
But this is what she eat:

Hunnie's fingers had already relaxed their grip on his mother's shirtwaist. He allowed Maggie Rose to wipe his tears.

A dozen raw, a plate of slaw,
A chicken and a roast,
Some sparrow grass, with apple sass,
And soft-shell crabs on toast.

On Maggie Rose's lap, Hunnie perched forward, his lips twitching as they tried to catch the rapid words, his face lighting with eagerness for his one line.

A big box stew with crackers too,
Her hunger was immense,
When she asked for pie I thought I'd die . . .

"FOR I HAD BUT FIFTY CENTS!" Hunnie yelled, and all the Kerners cheered.

"That was swell, Hunnie," Karl told him.

"Right on the beat," Kathleen said.

Hunnie fell happily against his mother as Hugo asked, "Which song next?"

Straightening to peer into the shadows of the Culleys' yard below them, Kathleen asked, "Is that Jame over there?"

"Looks like it," Karl answered. "He must be feeling better." On their way home—their mother insisted that Karl walk Kathleen home from the nickelodeon movie theater every night after it closed at nine—he'd told her everything that had happened that day, although he'd left out the part where Jame had mentioned her name. With his new awareness that Jame was probably sweet on Kathleen, Karl had searched for a reaction from his sister, but if there was one, she'd kept it hidden.

"Jame's lighting fireworks for the three little Marys," Kathleen told them. Her words were followed by staccato bursts from a string of penny firecrackers.

"Hasn't got sense enough to stay in bed and let his thick skull mend," Maggie Rose snorted. "He's as fool-headed as the rest of the Culleys."

Hugo said, "Now, Maggie Rose," but she only sniffed.

Kathleen and Karl exchanged glances, both of them hoping that their mother would let it go, would not spoil the grace of the summer evening with her opinion about the worthlessness of all Culleys. She'd already had plenty to say about Karl losing his job because of Jame.

Not that Maggie Rose was eager for Karl to go into the mills—on the contrary, she'd urged him to stay in school at least until his sixteenth birthday. It just galled her that Jame Culley had caused Karl to be fired. She counted it as one more proof that the Culleys were a curse to the Kerners.

Hugo had sympathized with Karl over the fact that every foreman in the steel mills could fire any man at whim, while the workingmen were powerless to protest. "But why worry about losing this job, son?" he'd asked. "You'll be a steelworker soon enough, and once you start, you'll be a steelworker all your life. So you might as well enjoy these few months before you turn sixteen. I would, if I were you."

Neither of Karl's parents seemed to realize how the mills lured him. Even the flame-tinted darkness overhead made him long to be a part of steelmaking, an industry so mighty it could change the color of the whole night sky. From the moment of his birth he'd heard the throb of the mills; it was as much a part of him as the sound of his heart beating beneath his skin. Now he was primed to enter the steelworks, to work his way into its vast vitality, become one of the men who made it live. He didn't want to wait four and a half more months!

Hugo raised his harmonica to begin "I'll Take You Home Again, Kathleen," his wife's favorite song. The second line was interrupted by the whoosh of a skyrocket. In the yard below, Mary Eileen, Mary Agnes, and Mary Frances Culley squealed with delight. Hunnie got off his mother's lap and walked to the side of the porch to watch the rocket flower in gold overhead, but the song went on without him—Hunnie didn't know all the words, anyway.

Karl watched his mother, her back turned resolutely, as she refused to look at the skyrocket because it came from the

Culleys' yard. Hugo swung into "When You and I Were Young, Maggie," a song he knew would improve his wife's ill-humor.

Hugo and Maggie Rose Kerner were a marriage of mixtures: he Lutheran, she Catholic; Hugo born in America of German parents, Maggie Rose Hannon stepping off the boat from Ireland when she was just sixteen. Hugo was easygoing, while Maggie Rose had a hot temper and could cling to a grudge bitterly for years, as she had done against the Culleys. Yet as unalike as they were, Hugo and Maggie Rose fit well together.

After the Culley fireworks ended, Hunnie climbed back onto his mother's lap. Following their custom, each of the Kerners took a turn requesting a favorite song.

In the pauses between their singing, Karl had been making up lines for a song to amuse his family. Hastily he ran the words through his head during the few snatches of quiet, because it was impossible for him to compose while everyone was singing something else. Karl intended to save his song for last, as a finale to his disastrous day—he needed the solace of the warm response he knew he'd get from his family.

When Hunnie began to yawn and rub his eyes, Maggie Rose said, "Time to sign off. This little muggins needs his bed. He's up long past his bedtime."

"I'll take him upstairs," Karl told her. "But first I want to sing something special. Pop, play the music for 'I Took My Girl to a Fancy Ball.'"

Hugo played a few bars of the chorus to lead into the song, and all eyes turned toward Karl. Each member of his family was smiling, leaning slightly forward, ready to approve his effort before they even heard it. Karl loved to perform for them, to have their fond attention center on him. He began:

> I went into the rolling mill,
> One hot Fourth of July,
> I took some sandwiches of ham
> And Mother's apple pie,
> I moved three tons of heavy steel,
> I was a working man,
> But when the day was over
> I got thrown out on my can.

For a second he tasted bitterness with the last lines, but then his family's cheers and applause washed over him like a benediction.

"That's the spirit, son," Hugo said, patting Karl's back. "I told you that someday you'd be able to laugh about what happened today. And here you are, laughing already. Sounds as though you've got over your disappointment pretty quick, am I right?"

No, Karl thought, his father wasn't right at all.

✦ ✦ ✦ ✦ ✦ ✦ ✦ ✦ ✦ ✦

CHAPTER TWO

HEATING

1

"I'm just about ready to give up," Jame said. He was leaning on the Kerners' back gate, with his forearms resting on the horizontal bar the pickets were nailed to. His muscular shoulders strained the cloth of his shirt.

"I been to every mill up and down the valley," Jame told Karl. "McKeesport, Clairton, Braddock, Homestead—I even went all the way to Pittsburgh. No one's hiring. This is the worst summer slump I can ever remember."

"I know," Karl answered as he picked up a trowel from inside the woodshed and kicked shut the door. "Two weeks ago I gave up trying to sneak into a man job, and decided to settle for a boy job. But no luck. I can't even land one of them. Jobs are so scarce it made me wonder how I ever got hired at Firth Sterling for that one day."

Jame moved his arms to make the gate squeak rhythmically, a peaceful sound in the early August morning. "You got hired because Baldy Weitz was trying to rush out the orders to get rid of the backlog. Management promised him a bonus if he could clear out the orders fast, 'cause they wanted to shut down the eight-inch mill for a while. Big John Reilly told me that last week when I ran into him at McToole's Bar."

"So my job wouldn't have lasted anyway, even if I hadn't been fired?" Karl asked.

"Nope. The only one of the gang from the eight-inch mill who's still working is Dutch Schwenk, wouldn't you know. They moved him over to the ten-inch mill. The rest of 'em have been laid off. They don't know when they're gonna get called back—prob'ly not for a couple weeks, at least."

Next door, the Culleys' screen door thumped shut as Bridey Culley came onto her porch carrying a clothes basket full of clean white linens. Looking around, she called, "Jame, where'd ye get to, lad? That clothesline's not all the way up yet, and I'm ready to hang."

"Got to go help my ma, Karl," Jame said, moving down the alley. "See you around."

Trowel in hand, Karl knelt among the rows of tomato plants in his mother's garden, enjoying the heavy scent that clung to his fingers after he touched their leaves. A few of the tomatoes were ripening into orange globes, vivid against the soot-specked green leaves. He began to weed around them, then paused to watch the activity in the Culleys' yard below.

One of the three little Marys unwound a ball of clothes-line as she trailed behind Jame, who pulled the line taut to tie it around a pole. Bridey Culley set down the clothes basket and straightened to rub her back, calling, "Francis X! Where the divil is that scamp? Come along and watch if there's an ore slip, Francis X." Wherever he was, Francis X Culley didn't show himself.

Karl observed with interest as Bridey and Jame pinned pair after pair of men's drawers onto the line. He knew that Bridey did all the laundry from the general superintendent's mansion overlooking the mill. Charles Bonner, the general superintendent of the Canaan Works of the Carnegie Steel Company, was the closest thing to royalty the town of Canaan, Pennsylvania, could boast, and it amused Karl to get a look at the great man's underwear. So many pairs of drawers hung on the line that Charles Bonner must have changed his underwear every single day.

As Bridey returned to her house with the empty basket, she patted the cheek of Mary Margaret, who was coming out the back door. "Mind now, lovey, do a good job of work," Bridey told her daughter, her voice carrying clearly to where Karl knelt. "God only knows we need the wages you're bringin' in."

Mary Margaret smiled at her mother. The long-sleeved black shirtwaist and long black skirt Mary Margaret wore made her thin frame look funereal and robbed her of any youthfulness. Yet Mary Margaret was lucky to have been hired as a maid in the general superintendent's mansion. The Culleys had fallen on harder than usual times after Jame lost his job, and her small wages helped them survive.

On her way to the back gate, Mary Margaret turned her eyes toward the Kerners' yard, but Karl ducked down in the tomato plants so he wouldn't have to speak to her. Since he'd found out she was sweet on him, Karl had carefully avoided any contact with her.

"Francis X, where the hell are you?" Jame bellowed from his yard. "Come here and watch for an ore slip."

Jame's bellow brought a sullen Francis X out of the outhouse. Scowling, the boy stationed himself at the highest point of the Culleys' yard, his gaze fastened on the mill's four blast furnaces, eighty feet tall, whose tops were visible from where Francis X sat. Judging by the dirty, ragged clothes Francis X wore, you'd never guess that his mother was a laundress, Karl thought. The boy's shirtwaist was torn and grimy, his pants too short even for short pants. In another year, when Francis X reached fourteen, the age at which boys graduated to long pants, his skinny legs would be fortunately hidden.

Karl moved to the rows of peas and weeded around them. As he worked, he dug his bare toes into the loosened soil, which was sun-warmed on top but cool and moist underneath. When he looked into the Culleys' yard again, after a quarter of an hour, he noticed his little brother, Hunnie, sitting next to Francis X, who wore a sly expression and was whispering something into Hunnie's ear that seemed to upset the little boy.

That dirty punk, Karl thought. If he's teasing my brother again, I'll wring his neck. But before Karl had a chance to holler for Hunnie to come home, a muffled explosion broke the morning stillness.

"Slip!" Francis X yelled at the top of his lungs. "Ma! Ore slip on D furnace."

From the top of the fourth blast furnace, a mixture of smoke, ore, and dust had shot a hundred feet into the sky. The orange-red column stood straight up for a moment, as though testing the direction of the wind, and then began to move lazily toward Chestnut Street and Pine Alley.

With a bang, the Culleys' screen door burst backward as Bridey, Jame, and the three little Marys swarmed into the yard, carrying empty clothes baskets. Given ordinary luck, they'd have ten minutes to get the wash off the line before the ore hit.

In a never-ending process, the huge, cylindrical blast furnaces were loaded from the top with alternate layers of coke, iron ore, and limestone. As the heat melted the ore, the load slowly sank, to be tapped out of the bottom as more coke, ore, and limestone were added through the top. Sometimes, though, a layer of ore would get stuck, welding itself to the sides of the furnace as the rest of the burden settled, widening a gap in the middle of the furnace. When the stuck ore broke loose and fell, it could drop with enough force to blow the tops off furnaces and kill steelworkers. Most often the ore slip only shot plumes of smoke into the sky, orange smoke that drifted outward and rained ore dust on fresh laundry.

Charles Bonner's wet drawers and table linens were hastily dumped into wicker baskets as the Culleys labored to get the wash inside. Karl debated whether he should help them, but they seemed to have the situation under control. After a moment he called, "Hunnie, come on home. Get over here before the dirt falls."

Hunnie came through the back gate, his feet scraping along the path, his face in a pout. Karl asked, "What's the matter? Was Francis X teasing you again? It looked like . . . " Hunnie walked right past him.

"Hunnie, I'm talking to you! Didn't you hear me? Answer me," Karl said. He followed his brother onto the back porch as particles of soot and ore began to fall silently, peppering the grass, garden, and path.

The little boy turned to face Karl. "Don't call me Hunnie," he said.

"What do you mean, don't call you Hunnie? Who are you supposed to be?"

"My real name is Henry," he answered. "That's who I'm supposed to be."

"Well, for Pete's sake, what brought this on? Did that Francis X...?"

"Hunnie is a girl's name," Henry declared.

"It is not. It's your own special nickname. Say, wait a minute, I bet you're thinking of Honey Kratzer. Honey is her nickname, just like Hunnie is yours, but they're spelled two different ways," Karl tried to explain. "I know you don't understand about spelling, Hunnie, but ..."

"My name is Henry!" he shouted, running through the back door into the kitchen.

Annoyed, Karl muttered, "That Francis X, I'll wipe up the street with him, putting stupid ideas into Hunnie's head like that." Karl liked the name Hunnie. He remembered when it had first been given to his baby brother.

It was one of the nights when his father's euchre club had met at the Kerner house. After the men finished playing cards, Maggie Rose set out platters of ham, cheese, and bread with one hand, holding six-month-old Hunnie in her other arm because he was fretful with his first tooth.

One of the euchre club members, an Englishman named Tommie Digman, had watched Maggie Rose and her baby with the sentimental expression bachelors sometimes wear around domestic scenes. "Look at that little chap," Tommie had said. "What a round, German head he has! He's a proper little Hun."

From then on the baby had been Hunnie. But now he wanted to be Henry. Well, he'd get over that. Karl wasn't going to change what he called his little brother just because Francis X razzed the kid.

When Karl went into the kitchen, Maggie Rose asked him, "Did you finish the weeding?"

"All done."

"Then I want you to go to the butcher shop for me. Get a pound and a half of boiling beef. You'd better put on your shoes, or the hot sidewalk will burn your feet."

"Nah," Karl answered. "My feet are all dirty. I'd have to wash them before I could put on my shoes, and I don't want to bother. I'll just go barefoot."

2

On his way into Heilmann's Butcher Shop, Karl noticed a pot of lead bubbling on one of the iron sidewalk doors that covered the entrance to Heilmann's cellar. The pot hung from a tripod; a blowtorch beneath it heated the lead. Karl figured some plumbers must be working in Heilmann's cellar, because plumbers used molten lead for repair jobs on broken pipes.

On his way out of the butcher shop, Karl had forgotten about the pot of lead boiling on the flat sidewalk door. One of the plumbers in the cellar must have forgotten about it, too—just at that moment the man came up the cellar stairs and raised the iron door from underneath. The blowtorch and tripod got knocked over, and the falling pot sprayed a thin layer of molten lead onto Karl's bare toes.

Screaming from the shock of scalding lead on his skin, Karl hopped on his undamaged foot while the lead solidified between his toes. The plumber's astonished face appeared above the edge of the door, and Karl, ashamed to have the man see him crying, ran across Canaan Avenue to begin the long climb up Center Street.

Although the lead had cooled quickly, the burning in Karl's toes hurt worse each minute. He moaned out loud as he hobbled up the hill on the heel of his left foot. The distance from Heilmann's to his home was a quarter mile; by the time Karl limped through his kitchen door, cold sweat mingled with the tears on his face.

"Mother of God!" Maggie Rose leaped from her chair, scattering the potful of peas she'd been shelling. "What happened to you?"

Grimacing with pain, Karl told about the plumbers, the cellar door, the boiling lead. In some surprise, he noticed he was still clutching the package of meat; he set it on the table. Kathleen and Hunnie had come running at the commotion, and stared wide-eyed at the lead that fused Karl's toes with a solid metal coating.

"Oh, my darlin', we'll have to get it off, and it's going to hurt something awful," Maggie Rose cried. "Here, sit on the chair. I'll wash the dirt off your foot first."

She set a tin basin in the sink and half-filled it from the single faucet, then added hot water from a kettle that always stood on the back of the stove. With a washrag and soap she lathered Karl's soot-stained sole, then gently lifted his foot into the basin to rinse it. Mercifully, the layer of lead kept the soap and water from reaching his burned skin.

"Here, lift your foot onto the table," his mother told him. Starting with his little toe, she began to pull away the hardened lead, wincing because the skin came off with it. Karl let out a cry, and Hunnie began to whimper.

"Hunnie shouldn't be seeing this," Maggie Rose said. "Kathleen, take him down the alley to the Kratzers and ask Mrs. Kratzer if he can stay there for an hour or two."

After they'd gone, Maggie Rose went to work on Karl's other toes. The removal of the lead was far more painful than the scalding had been, because the metal had fused itself so tightly to the skin that there was no way to get it off without taking skin, too. Karl groaned as each bit came off, and Maggie Rose wept at the pain she was causing him. When Kathleen returned, Maggie Rose told her, "Hold your brother's hand tight. Karl, squeeze Kathleen's fingers as hard as you can. It will help ease the pain."

As carefully as she could, wiping the tears from her own eyes so that she could see better, Maggie Rose worked patiently until all the bits of lead had been removed and lay on the floor, showing perfect molds of Karl's toes. He sat through the ordeal with his eyes shut tight and his teeth clenched to keep from crying out, squeezing Kathleen's hand in a grip he knew must hurt, although Kathleen bore it without trying to pull away. When he opened his eyes, the sight of the discarded lead, and of the raw flesh on his toes, made Karl's stomach lurch.

Maggie Rose spread carbolic salve over his foot and wrapped strips of torn sheet around his toes, while Kathleen swept the bits of lead and the scattered peas into the dustpan.

After she'd made Karl comfortable with a pillow under his foot, Maggie Rose straightened her back. And straightened it farther.

Her expression began to change from concern to wrath. A red flush rose to her cheeks as fire glinted from her eyes. "How dare they!" she cried. "How *dare* they do this to my child!"

Maggie Rose tore off her apron and threw it onto the kitchen table. "Kathleen, get my hat! We're going right down there and tell those people what we think of them."

"Who's going?" Kathleen asked.

"I am going, and you are going."

"Me? Why do I have to go?"

"Because I want you to keep the plumbers from running away while I give the butcher a piece of my mind. After I'm finished with the butcher, I'll get to the plumbers!"

Kathleen sputtered, "Mom, how am I supposed to . . . ?"

"You'll do as I say!" Maggie Rose yelled. "Now get my hat!"

When Kathleen came running with her mother's black summer straw, Maggie Rose jammed it squarely on her head and jabbed the hat pin with such force that Karl thought she'd puncture her scalp. "Just wait till I get my hands on that Heilmann," she stormed.

"It wasn't Heilmann's fault," Karl protested.

"It was his cellar, was it not? And we're always paying our bill on time, that's the devil of it." Chin jutting like the prow of a ship, Maggie Rose sailed through the back door in a fury of maternal outrage, dragging Kathleen behind her.

Karl's pain had eased enough that he could smile at the spectacle of his mother's full-blown Irish temper, and sympathize over the fate that awaited poor Adolph Heilmann, the butcher. He stayed seated at the kitchen table, debating whether he should get up to put the meat in the icebox, but deciding it was wiser not to walk anywhere if he didn't have to.

A small, worn book lay on the tabletop. *How to Talk Cor-*

rectly, it was titled. Twenty-three years earlier, Maggie Rose had received it from her sister Mae, when they were on the boat bound for America. Both of them had been concerned that their Irish brogues would keep them from finding jobs as maids in the new country. The book had taught Maggie Rose to speak with refinement—only when she was deeply disturbed did she lapse into a bit of brogue. She still studied the book from time to time. Though she hadn't had much formal education, Maggie Rose believed that a person could continue to learn.

The little book made Karl think of school. He wondered whether his toes might stay sore enough that he wouldn't be able to wear shoes for a month or so. Surely his mother wouldn't make him go to school if he couldn't put on a shoe. Maybe he could use that as an excuse to stay out of school until his birthday in November. By that time the mills would surely be hiring again.

Carefully, he tested his toes to see whether they hurt unbearably if he wiggled them. They hurt, but not unbearably. School was exactly a month away, and Karl had a good hunch his toes would have healed by that time. Shoot! It was a shame to go through so much pain if he couldn't get any advantage out of it, like weasling out of school.

Not that Karl hated school particularly. It was just that for as long as he could remember, he'd wanted to be a steelworker. When he was a little kid, he would run down Pine Alley each evening his father had been working day turn, excited to meet Hugo on his way home from work. After catching Karl in his arms for a hug, Hugo would open his dinner pail to take out a treat he'd saved for Karl—half an apple, a couple of crackers, or a hard-boiled egg. It didn't matter what the treat was, Karl loved it because it had come out of his father's dinner pail, which had been with his father inside the mill where his father made steel. Hugo, dressed in soot-blackened work clothes, was far more heroic to Karl than the president of the United States dressed in striped pants and a silk hat.

Karl had applied himself in school to learn all the reading, writing, and arithmetic he would need for a job as a steelworker. That was fine, and he'd been willing. But the classes he'd be forced to take in his sophomore year—literature, algebra, history—would do him no good whatsoever in the mills. Maggie Rose had told him in no uncertain terms, though, that she wouldn't put up with his loafing around the house from the beginning of September until his sixteenth birthday. So he was to go to school, she said, and learn as much as he could until he was old enough for a man job.

Karl shrugged. He'd have to make the best of it somehow, endure the boredom until he'd served his term and could finally escape to the mills on November twentieth. Then at last he would become a workingman.

Forty-five minutes had passed before Karl heard his mother stomp across the back porch so loudly that he knew her anger hadn't altogether cooled.

"I want to hear all about it," Karl told Kathleen as Maggie Rose marched across the kitchen and plunked into her rocking chair next to the window. Her back was straight as a yardstick, her hat still firmly in place.

"Well, you should have been there, Karl," Kathleen said. "Adolph Heilmann never had a fighting chance, the poor guy. Want to see how it went? Pretend you're at the nickelodeon watching a movie called *How the Irish Beat the Huns at the Battle of Heilmann's Butcher Shop.*"

Kathleen picked up her mother's apron from the table and wrapped it around her, prepared to act out the scene for Karl. Twisting her face in mock fear, she deepened her voice to mimic Heilmann.

"Oh, missus," she cried, "I feel awful, chust awful! Ven I ran out to help Karl, he vass gone already."

Whipping the apron behind her, Kathleen became Maggie Rose. "Do ye know what ye did to my poor boy, ye hound?" she said, in a perfect imitation of her mother's angry brogue. "Not a cent more of my money will ye ever get, ye dirty blackguard!"

Heilmann again, Kathleen deepened her voice. "Here, missus, take home a nice pork roast. Free! Take a summer sausage. Please take! Leaf me make it up to you. Chust giff me a chance."

"I wouldn't touch your filthy meat for all the tea in China," Kathleen as Maggie Rose cried, shaking her fist. "Do ye think ye can buy me? Just wait till my mister hears o' this. He'll give ye the back of his hand, he will."

Karl roared with laughter at Kathleen's mimicry, and noticed his mother's cheeks twitch with the effort not to smile.

In her own voice, Kathleen said, "So then Mom took after him with a meat cleaver and Heilmann locked himself in the cooler . . . ."

"Oh, Kathleen," Maggie Rose broke in, smiling now, "such foolish blather! I did no such thing, Karl."

"What about the plumbers?" Karl asked. "Tell me that part."

"They were long gone by the time we got there," Kathleen answered. "Someone must have warned them that Maggie Rose Kerner was coming after them to bash in their heads with a wrench."

"Kathleen, the way you exaggerate!" Maggie Rose said, laughing as she tried to keep her dignity. "It must be from all those movies you watch at the nickelodeon. Glory be to God!" Her mouth dropped in consternation. "I just thought of something! Who's going to walk you home tonight from the nickelodeon? Karl can't, and Pop can't."

Because it was a Saturday, the night of shift change, Hugo Kerner would work straight through, his night turn beginning as the day turn ended, so that when he got off at six the next morning, he would have worked twenty-four hours in the open hearth, without sleep. Then, after just twelve hours rest, he'd report for work again at six Sunday evening.

"For heaven's sake, Mom, I can walk home by myself," Kathleen said. "I'd better get used to it—from the looks of that foot, Karl won't be able to come after me for quite some time."

"Absolutely not! No decent girl walks alone at night," Maggie Rose declared. At Kathleen's frown, she went on, "Ah, darlin', it's not that I worry over what people would say. It's only that I wouldn't draw an easy breath if you were outside by yourself in the dark."

"What about Andy?" Karl suggested.

Maggie Rose brightened. "Of course. We could ask Andy Stulak to go after Kathleen every night until your foot gets better, Karl. I'll give Andy a nickel every time. Do you think he'd do it?"

"As soon as he gets home from work," Karl said, "I'll go over and ask him."

"You'd better not," his mother fretted. "Your foot's much too sore."

"Mom, if I could make it all the way up Center Street right

after I got burned, I think I can make it as far as next door, even if I have to hop on one foot."

3

"Mom," Karl called from the Stulaks' back porch, "Andy's mother invited me to eat supper over here."

He waited, hoping, until his mother poked her head around the back door. "Well, if you're sure it's no bother to Mrs. Stulak," she called back, "it would be fine with me, because I haven't even started our supper."

"Thanks, Mom." Karl was happy she'd agreed. He loved to eat at the Stulaks'—Mrs. Stulak was a wonderful cook. "And Andy says he'll go after Kathleen, so don't worry about that."

In the Stulaks' backyard, the two boarders, Vaclav and Emil Hrenko, were stripped to the waist, soaping away the grime of the mill in a washtub set on an upended box. They were brothers who'd come to America only a year before. Since both were unmarried and had no need for a house of their own, they paid the Stulaks for a room and their meals. Almost all the new immigrants started out that way—as boarders—until they either married in America or brought their women over from the old country.

Andy had gone to the end of the yard to fill the coal scuttle, so Karl limped into the Stulaks' kitchen, inhaling deeply because the kitchen was filled with delicious odors. "Vitajce u nas," Mrs. Stulak welcomed Karl. She said something else in Slovak to her daughter Veronica, who had already set six plates on the table. Veronica added a seventh.

Karl sat on a kitchen chair watching Mrs. Stulak drop pirohis into a pot of boiling water—they were his favorite of all the Slovak dishes. Mrs. Stulak was as round a dumpling as the pirohis. Her thin hair was drawn into a tight bun; her eyes blinked rapidly because they watered too much. When he was little, Karl had thought that Mrs. Stulak's eyes watered because her hair was pulled too tight.

"Good!" Karl told her, pointing to the pirohis in the pot. Since Mrs. Stulak could speak no English at all, she and Karl communicated mostly in smiles and nods. "Good pirohis," he said. She chuckled at his pronunciation of the word.

Soon all of them were seated around the table, the men wearing clean, collarless shirts. Andy's father and the boarder Vaclav Hrenko let their suspenders hang around their hips, but the younger Hrenko brother, Emil, had his suspenders where they belonged, his hair neatly combed, and his fingernails painstakingly cleaned, because he was in love with Veronica Stulak. They were going to be married.

During the meal, Andy's father seemed worried and distracted. When he'd finished eating, he sat with his chin pressed gloomily against his hands.

Three pirohis remained in the bowl; Mrs. Stulak offered them to Karl. As Karl spooned the pirohis onto his plate, Mr. Stulak pointed a finger at him and made an angry-sounding comment in Slovak.

"Bohze moj!" his wife exclaimed, looking shocked. The others sat motionless, in silence, but Andy's cheeks flamed. Mrs. Stulak answered her husband in an angry voice while Veronica looked disdainful, Emil embarrassed, and Vaclav amused.

Karl set his fork down without tasting the remaining pirohis, realizing that the argument had something to do with him and the pirohis, even though the whole quarrel took place in Slovak. After shouting something at his father, Andy jumped up from the table, knocking his chair backward. Without bothering to pick it up, he grabbed Karl's arm and said, "Let's get out of here." He flung open the screen door and stomped across the back porch.

"Andrej!" his father shouted after him, but Andy kept going, and his father didn't call again.

Karl hobbled after Andy all the way to the end of the backyard, where Andy threw himself to the ground underneath the apple tree.

"He makes me so dang mad!" Andy raged, his cheeks still flaming.

"What was it all about?" Karl asked.

"Nothing," Andy snapped. "Absolutely nothing."

The pirohis made a heavy lump inside Karl's stomach. "Andy, I know it was about me, so you'd better tell me."

"Cheap, stingy old man!" Andy smacked the tree trunk with his fist.

As Karl waited for Andy to explain, his worry increased. Occasionally, when he'd visited the Stulaks, he'd said or done something considered ill-bred in the Slovak culture. Always before, the Stulaks had laughed with good humor at Karl's unintentional errors.

"You didn't do anything wrong," Andy said, guessing Karl's concern. "Look, the way my father acted just now was disgusting. But I know what was gnawing at him, so I'll try to explain, even though there's no excuse for what he said."

Andy dug his fingers through his dark blond hair, rumpling it. "See, Karl, just before supper, Veronica and Emil told my old man that after they get married and move to a place of their own, Emil's brother Vaclav is going to board with them. That means my old man'll not only lose Veronica's wages from her job, but he'll lose both Emil's board and Vaclav's board, too."

When Karl looked puzzled, Andy said, "I guess you don't understand. Your pop has a good job and makes decent pay. My old man's a laborer. After eighteen years in the mill, he's still doing the same dumb job he started with. No promotions, because he's a hunky and can't speak English right. Anyway, the mills are slow just now, worse than just the usual summer slump, and my father's scared to death that he'll get laid off. He's trying to buy this house, and if he can't make the payments, he'll lose everything."

Searching Andy's face, because Andy never lied to him, Karl asked, "So what did your father say about me?"

Andy scowled. "He said you eat over at our house an awful lot, and if you want to keep on eating with us, you better start paying for your eats like the boarders do."

"Oh." Karl grew hot with embarrassment.

"Listen, that's just my old man, don't let it get to you," Andy said. "My mother told him off, believe me. She said if we can't provide hospitality for our friends, then we might as well be back in the old country starving to death. Please, Karl, I only told you because you asked me. Promise it won't make any difference between us."

"It won't," Karl promised, but he knew he'd never go to the Stulaks' for supper again, no matter how often they invited him.

"It's this dang stupid way the mills are run," Andy went on bitterly. "The Irish and the Germans, and the Johnny Bulls, too, get all the good jobs. Slovaks like us can never be anything but laborers, and when the bad times come we get laid off and the so-called Americans take over our jobs till times get better."

Karl hadn't realized that. He tried to say something sympathetic, but Andy's words were building into a tirade.

"Do you know why my father's the way he is—so scared about money and about losing his job?" Andy demanded. "It's because of the Homestead strike twenty years ago. My father was new in this country then, and he believed all that crap about democracy. He thought nothing could be more democratic than a union, so he talked all the Slovaks he knew into striking to support the union. Know what he got for his trouble?" Andy's voice had risen with emotion. "He got trampled under the hooves of a policeman's horse. He got two broken legs, and he got fired from his job. He couldn't get work again until he left Homestead and moved here to Canaan. And he got his spirit broken, because the things he believed in turned out to be big fakes."

Karl had never heard Andy speak that way before. He stared in silence as Andy went on, "Or maybe they aren't fakes. I think the union might have been a good thing for Slovaks like me, if it had ever gotten off the ground. But unionism's been dead since the Homestead strike. The men are either too scared to organize or else they're duped into thinking they're better off the way things are."

Andy's lips twisted in scorn. "Andrew Carnegie gives the town a big, beautiful public library and says to people like my father, 'See, don't I treat you good? Did you ever have anything like this in your village in the old country? So keep your mouth shut and be happy with the twelve lousy dollars and sixty cents a week you get paid.'" He cursed angrily.

"Jeez, Andy, don't get so hot under the collar," Karl said, but Andy hadn't finished.

"Sometimes I just want to get away from this lousy valley and go someplace where they won't call me hunky," he said. "A place that I could get a decent job and not be the first one laid off when work's slow."

Francis X Culley's head popped up above the Stulaks' back gate. "What's Andy talkin' about?" he asked.

"Francis X, beat it!" Karl yelled. "How long have you been there?"

"Long enough," Francis X replied. "What's bitin' Andy?"

"Get your nebby little nose out from where it doesn't belong," Karl told him. "Go on home."

Unperturbed, Francis X asked, "You guys want to play ball when Andy gets through yellin'?"

"Can't you see I have a sore foot?" Karl asked, raising his bandaged toes. "Now scram, you little ..."

Karl bit his tongue on the name he'd been about to call Francis X, because he saw Jame Culley climbing the alley toward them. Francis X might be a royal pain in the behind, but he was, after all, Jame's brother.

"Francis X," Jame called, "Ma wants you to come home and wipe the dishes."

"Ah, why don't you wipe them?" Francis X whined. "You ain't workin' now, so you oughta help Ma once in a while."

Jame roared, "You little snot, you shut your trap before I paste you one! I been helping Ma all day while you kept weasling out of your chores."

Dodging Jame's upraised arm, Francis X sidled down the alley toward home. Jame leaned on the gate and sighed. "I don't know how I'm ever gonna make a man out of that little punk," he said. "What's goin' on with you two?"

Subdued, Andy asked, "Do you have any idea what time it is, Jame?"

"Pretty close to eight, I think. Why?"

"In about half an hour, I have to go to the nickelodeon to pick up Kathleen."

Jame straightened. "Oh. Yeah. I heard about Karl's foot from . . . someone. Cripes, Karl, first my head gets bashed, and now your foot gets fried. It's been a great summer." Jame paused, and then, as though he were trying to sound casual, said, "So you're going after Kathleen, huh, Andy?"

"Yep. Mrs. Kerner said she'd pay me a nickel each time I go until Karl's foot gets better, but I don't want to take any money just for doing a friend a favor."

Jame shifted his weight. "You know, ever since I heard about Karl, I been kinda thinkin'. How 'bout if I go and get Kathleen? Not just tonight, but every night. I mean, I don't want the money either. You keep it, Andy. I just want the chance to walk Kathleen home."

Jame's unexpected request made Karl squirm, made him wonder how he could answer without hurting Jame's feelings. "It would be a great idea, Jame," he said slowly, "except . . . you know how my mom . . ."

"Yeah, I know your mother hates all us Culleys, but she wouldn't have to know, would she? See, Andy could start out like he was going to the nickelodeon, and then he could go somewheres else instead. I know Kathleen wouldn't say anything to your mom, and I can trust you two fellows, 'cause you're my pal, right, Karl? You, too, Andy," he added as an afterthought.

How can you be so sure Kathleen wouldn't say anything, Karl was tempted to ask, but he didn't.

Andy shrugged. "Makes no difference to me. But if you're going to walk her home while Karl's foot's sore, you should get the nickels, Jame."

Jame looked outraged. "Take money for walking a lady home? What kind of a sap do you think I am?"

"Cool down, Jame. I didn't mean anything," Andy told him. "What kind of a sap do you think I'd be if I took money without doing the job?"

"I know the answer," Karl said. "You take the nickels, Andy, and save them. When Veronica marries Emil, we'll use the money to buy them a wedding present."

"Does that mean it's all right with you if I walk your sister home?" Jame asked Karl.

Karl realized that he was being made responsible for the decision—Jame wouldn't go if Karl objected. God help me if I'm doing the wrong thing, he prayed. "Sure, go ahead if you want to, Jame," he said.

Grinning broadly, Jame said, "Nifty! I'll start out right now. When it's time, Andy, you walk down the hill like you're going to the nickelodeon. Then, about nine-thirty, me and Kathleen will meet you on the middle dip of Center Street. No, wait, there's a street light there, so make it the dip below that."

Andy agreed, and Jame left, whistling as he walked down Pine Alley. "So that's how things are with Jame, huh?" Andy asked Karl. "He likes your sister."

"I guess so. But I don't know how Kathleen feels about Jame," Karl replied. "She never lets on. What are you going to do with yourself, Andy, while you're supposed to be going after Kathleen every night? You can't hang around here, or someone will see you and figure out what's happening."

Andy plucked a blade of grass and wound it around his finger. "Oh . . . I'll just take some little walks along Oak Street," he answered.

"Oak Street? Why Oak Street?"

Andy placed the blade of grass between his thumbs and blew on it, changing its position until he produced a loud whistle. "Do you know Virginia Ward?" he asked.

Karl nodded. Of course he knew Virginia Ward. She'd been in his ninth-grade class last year.

"Well, about a month ago, I was coming home from the library one night about nine o'clock, and I cut across Oak Street. The Wards have this big dog, see, and that night Virginia came out to let the dog off its chain and give it some water. So I went back that way a couple of times after that, and sure enough, every night at nine Virginia comes out to take care of the dog."

"Andy!" Karl exclaimed. "Are you stuck on Virginia Ward?" Looking sheepish, Andy said, "Stuck? I don't know. Maybe. I guess so. I think she's a good looker, don't you?"

Virginia Ward was blond, dimpled, and giggly, with about as much sense as a feather quilt, Karl thought. "Did you ever talk to her?" he asked.

Andy replied, "When I go past, I say hello and she says hello. I don't know, Karl, I kind of have the feeling that if I had the nerve to say more, she wouldn't mind, maybe. Only, I'd have to be careful. If Harry Ward saw a hunky talking to his daughter, he'd kick my dupa all the way down Oak Street to the Monongahela River."

Karl had to agree. Harry Ward was the mayor of Canaan,

Pennsylvania, or P.A. as people called it because P.A. was easier to say than Pennsylvania. Local talk had it that Ward might run for state senator after another term as mayor. Andy's opinion of the man was right on the mark: Although Harry Ward wanted the votes of the few immigrants who'd become naturalized citizens, he certainly didn't think of them as his social equals.

"Well, I guess I'd better get started," Andy said, ducking his head as he stood to keep from hitting the low branches of the apple tree. "I have a library book that's due tomorrow, so I might as well take it back before I ... well, see you later, Karl."

Andy went into his house and returned with the book, then waved to Karl as he left the yard. Karl stayed under the Stulaks' apple tree as darkness deepened around him. The tart scent of the unripe apples almost offset the smoke smell from the mills.

An epidemic of romance seemed to have broken loose in the neighborhood, Karl reflected. Emil Hrenko and Veronica Stulak: That one seemed natural. Jame and Kathleen: Trouble ahead there, in the shape of Maggie Rose Kerner, if anything should come of that romance. Andy and Virginia Ward– impossible, for the exact reason Andy had stated.

Karl's mind, listing the names of couples, didn't stop at three, but added his own name to the list. Karl and ... who? Certainly not Mary Margaret Culley, even though Jame had said she was sweet on Karl. Never Mary Margaret! If Karl ever took an interest in any girl–and until then the idea hadn't really occurred to him–she would be someone soft and rounded, not a skinny scarecrow like Mary Margaret Culley.

Yet ... Emil Hrenko was in love with Veronica Stulak, and Veronica was thin, with more angles to her than curves.

Looks aside, when Karl was ready to fall in love, he'd want a girl who had some fire in her, like his mother, Maggie Rose. He had to smile, thinking about five-foot-tall Maggie Rose bawling out the burly butcher, Adolph Heilmann.

Yet . . . Jame Culley, who could take his pick of any single woman in Canaan, P.A., and probably a few of the married ones, too, was sweet on Kathleen, who was clever and pretty, but not anywhere near as spunky as her mother.

And Andy! What could Andy see in that giddy Virginia Ward? Serious, intelligent Andy, who'd read almost every book in the Carnegie Free Public Library, falling for Virginia Ward! She couldn't even finish a sentence without giggling.

The whole notion of romantic love baffled Karl. Baffled him, but suddenly intrigued him, too. Maybe it would be nice to fall in love.

4

Three weeks and one day after the first time Jame walked Kathleen home, Hugo and Maggie Rose Kerner went on their monthly jaunt to Pittsburgh.

It was a Sunday, the day of shift change. Hugo had finished his night turn at 6:00 A.M. and would have twenty-four free hours before he began the day shift on Monday morning. After Hugo reached home, washed, breakfasted, and fell into bed, Maggie Rose and the children walked to 7:00 Mass at Holy Name Church. On their return, the Kerner children kept as quiet as possible to allow their father his rest, until Maggie Rose awakened her sleep-drugged husband at two in the afternoon.

One Sunday each month, on one of Hugo's every-two-week days of rest, he and his wife put on their best clothes and boarded the streetcar for downtown Pittsburgh. There they dined in what they felt was elegance at Dutch Henry's, always beginning the meal with oyster stew. Afterward they strolled along Fifth Avenue and peered through the lighted windows of department stores at displays of household furnishings and stylish clothes they would never buy, and didn't want a great deal, but enjoyed looking at.

Kathleen and Karl were left at home to take care of Hunnie. On that Sunday, August 25, for the better part of an hour, Karl fooled around at the piano. He started out playing "Alexander's Ragtime Band," and then, just for the fun of it, made up some variations on the tune and tempo. When he grew bored with that, Karl looked around for Kathleen and Hunnie, realizing that he'd seen neither of them for quite some time.

They weren't in the backyard, which was silent in the Sunday heat except for the thump of a ripe tomato that fell from its stem. Karl went upstairs to check the beds. Sometimes, when he'd been pulled awake and dressed for early Mass, Hunnie fell asleep by late afternoon. The beds were empty, though, except for a book lying on Kathleen's bed. Karl was tempted to pick up the book and read a bit of it because its title impressed him—*The Woman Beautiful: Maidenhood, Marriage, Maternity*. He left the book where it lay, though, because the topic was too intimidating.

By the time the kitchen clock showed ten to six, Karl began to worry. His mother had left cold meat, pickles, bread, and oranges for their supper. If Hunnie and Kathleen had gone somewhere together, they should have returned by then, brought home by hunger even if they didn't realize how late it was.

Karl walked through the backyard calling Hunnie's name,

but Hunnie didn't answer. Instead, Francis X Culley hollered, "He ain't over at our place. I seen him going down the alley about a hour ago."

"Was Kathleen with him?" Karl asked.

"No. I seen her going the same way, but that was a long time before Hunnie went."

Karl felt annoyed. Hunnie had probably sneaked into the grounds of the general superintendent's mansion again to look at the fish. The general superintendent's estate was off-limits to everyone, but Hunnie was fascinated by the huge goldfish swimming in the mosaic-tiled pool on the grounds. And why wasn't Kathleen watching him? She must have left the house long before, without saying a word to either Karl or Hunnie, taking it for granted that Karl would tend his little brother.

He hurried down Center Street to the second dip, then turned up the broad drive that led to the general superintendent's mansion. Halfway along its length, the graveled drive was blocked by a tall iron gate, but every kid in the neighborhood knew that farther up the long row of hedges that bordered the grounds, a thin spot in the hedge could be crawled through to get inside. Growing more irritated, Karl got down on his hands and knees and pushed his way through the tight hole in the hedge.

Inside, he looked around quickly to see whether the grounds-keeper was in sight. No one was visible, but Karl heard the cough of a motor, and barely had time to duck behind a rose arbor before the general superintendent's automobile chugged down the driveway from the mansion.

Charles Bonner sat alone in the back seat of his big Franklin Landaulet. Feeling fairly confident that he couldn't be seen, Karl peered out through the roses to admire the shiny brass headlamps of the motor car, the rubber bulb horn he would have loved to squeeze, the tall steering wheel he would have loved to turn. Bonner's chauffeur stopped the automobile and climbed down from the front seat to open the gate, then drove through and locked the gate behind them. As the car drove away, Karl stepped from behind the roses to yearn after it. The shiny blue chassis was set so high on the wheels that it looked more like a royal coach than an automobile.

Since Charles Bonner and the chauffeur had left, the grounds-keeper was probably slipping off somewhere to sneak a nap or a pint of beer, so Karl felt less concern about being caught.

He headed in the direction of the fishpond. Sunlight and leaf shadows patterned the water's surface, but Hunnie was not lying belly-down, his usual position, at the edge of the pond.

Where could he be? It had been more than an hour since Francis X had seen him. A terrible fear stopped Karl's breath as he ran to the pond and stared into the water, because Hunnie might have slipped and fallen in. But the water, clear except for dots of soot on its surface, held only fat orange fish.

Karl couldn't holler for Hunnie in the superintendent's grounds—one of the servants might hear him. There was no need to, anyway, because nothing on the estate interested Hunnie except the fishpond. Karl squirmed backward through the hedge and climbed Center Street, calling for Hunnie loudly. All the way up Pine Alley he shouted Hunnie's name, listening for an answer but hearing none.

"Din't you find him yet?" Francis X asked when Karl passed the Culleys'.

"No. I don't know where he's gone to."

"I'll come help you look," Francis X said. "After we find Hunnie, do you want to play ball?"

"Huh-uh, not today," Karl answered.

"Is your foot still sore?"

No, Karl's foot was no longer sore. He was able to wear shoes, so he'd have to go to school when it started, unfortunately. And he'd soon have to admit to his mother that he could start walking Kathleen home from the nickelodeon. Jame would be disappointed, but Karl would be relieved when the whole deception was over.

"My foot's better now, but I don't want to play ball," Karl told Francis X.

"I betcha if that hunky wanted you to play with him, you would," Francis X said accusingly.

"Francis X, you're just itching for a good punch in the snoot. If you don't stop calling Andy a hunky, I'll bash your nose so flat you'll have to breathe through your ears," Karl threatened.

"Well, gee whiz!" Francis X cried. "Andy calls his own self a hunky. I heard him sayin' it that night you two guys was talkin' in his yard."

Karl doubled his fist and raised it level with Francis X's nose. "Andy can say it if he wants to. You can't. Got that straight?"

"I got it! I got it! Holy gee." Francis X backed away, then yelled, "Hunnie! See, Karl, I'm helping you find him. Hunnie! Where you at?"

A half hour later, the three little Marys had joined the search, combing every yard and vacant lot between Pine Alley and Chestnut Street. The hill rang with calls of "Hunnie! Hunnie! Come home!"

Karl was growing desperate with worry. Could his little brother have gone all the way down to the mill, to the dangerous railroad yard? How could Karl face his parents if they came home at ten o'clock and Hunnie was still missing? And where had Kathleen gone off to? Why was Karl having to make the frightening search all by himself, with only the help of the Culley children?

Karl ran all the way down Center Street and then sprinted along the railroad tracks, terrified that he'd find Hunnie's body crumpled along the rails. He asked the few people he met whether they'd seen a five-year-old boy, but no one had.

As he ran back up Center Street, Karl trembled so hard that his legs staggered. If anything bad had happened to Hunnie—Karl panicked at the possibility.

After he'd checked every room in the house again—Hunnie might have returned home and fallen asleep while Karl was out looking for him—Karl ran through the backyard and banged on the door of the woodshed for the fourth time, yelling, "Hunnie!" in a cry that verged on a sob. Then, on an impulse, he opened the door of the shed.

Evening sunlight wedged through the door to fall on Hunnie's bare toes, Hunnie's hands clasped around his knees.

"Hunnie!" Karl roared. "Why didn't you answer? Didn't you hear everyone calling you?"

"I heard people calling Hunnie," the little boy replied. "That's not my name. My name's Henry."

Karl's terror turned to fury. He yanked Hunnie to his feet, unbuttoned his short pants from the back buttons of his shirtwaist, and smacked his bare backside again and again until Hunnie screamed with pain.

"Karl found him," he heard Francis X's voice call from the

alley. "He was in the woodshed. Karl's giving him a beating."

Realizing that he'd hit his little brother much too hard, Karl sank down on the floorboards and pulled the sobbing child into his arms. "Hunnie, you don't know how scared I was," Karl told him. His heart still pounded and his arms shook as he tried to hug the child.

Hunnie pulled away violently, his dirty face streaked with tears and red with rage. "My . . . name . . . is . . . HENRY!" he shouted through his sobs.

"All right, all right, I'll try to remember that from now on," Karl said, mentally cursing Francis X. "But do you know why Francis X told you Hunnie was a girl's name? Because *Francis* sounds the same as a girl's name. He even has a little sister named Mary Frances." Bridey Culley had such deep devotion to Saint Francis Xavier that she'd named two of her children after him.

"I don't care about that," Henry stuttered, his chest still heaving. "I keep telling people my name's Henry, but no one listens."

Karl drew his little brother into his arms again, resting his chin on top of Henry's head. The blond hair felt springy and stiff, and smelled of little-boy sweat and woodshed dust. Karl was overcome with love for his brother. He felt weak with relief that Henry was safe, and regretted that he'd hit him too hard.

"Where were you all afternoon, anyway?" Karl asked him.

"P . . . playing in Kratzer's yard with Honey. Then I didn't want to play with her anymore, so I came in here to hide from her." Relaxing a little, he curled against Karl.

"Hun . . . Henry," Karl said, "that was a terrible thing you did, not answering me when I was trying to find you. I was scared to death that something bad had happened to you. Do you know what it would do to our mom if you got hurt or . . . " Karl was going to say "killed," but caught himself. "Or lost?"

"No," Henry mumbled.

"Remember that song that always makes you cry? 'Always in the Way'? That's about a little kid whose mother died, and it makes you so sad you cry. But it's just as sad when a mother loses her children. Maybe even sadder."

"I'm not lost," Henry said. "I'm right here."

"Thank God for that. But Mom and Pop did lose two of their children. That's something you never knew about. That's why I was so scared when I couldn't find you—I didn't know what it would do to Mom if she lost another child." Or to him, if he lost another brother.

"Before you were born," Karl said, "I had a brother named Kurt. And another sister besides Kathleen. Her name was Kara"

"Why didn't anybody ever tell me?" Henry asked.

"We don't talk about them," Karl explained, "because it breaks Mom's heart."

Henry was silent for a moment, mulling over the strange revelation. Then he asked, "What were they like, your other brother and sister?"

"They were your brother and sister, too," Karl told him. "They were nice. Kurt was two years younger than me, and Kara was two years younger than Kurt."

"Did they look like me or like you?" Henry asked.

"Like you." Karl grew quiet, thinking back to the year before Henry's birth, when he'd been nine, Kurt seven, and Kara five. Kara—sweet, blond, a miniature Maggie Rose, but thin and delicate. Kurt, with the same blond coloring and the looks of an angel, full of energy and laughter, singing when he wasn't laughing at his own made-up games.

"How did they get lost?" Henry asked.

"They didn't get lost. They got sick and died. Kathleen and I were sick, too, but we got better. Kurt and Kara didn't."

Karl remembered it much too well, from the very beginning of the tragedy. The way Mary Eileen Culley had always come to the Kerner house to play with Kara, because even as a child of seven, Mary Eileen liked the cleanliness and order of the Kerner home better than the dirt and bedlam of the Culley house. Mary Eileen always brought along her little sister Mary Agnes, even on the day when Mary Agnes was coughing and feverish, a fact Maggie Rose didn't discover for more than an hour because she was doing the wash, and the children had played quietly in the parlor. It was not until Mary Agnes Culley began to cry hoarsely that her throat hurt that Maggie Rose sent her home.

A few days later, when Maggie Rose learned that the Culley children were severely ill with diphtheria, she became frantic. She sent for the doctor and put her own children to bed, but it didn't matter. She couldn't save them. One by one they took sick, Kara first, then Kurt, then Karl and Kathleen.

On the day that Karl awakened from a lingering red haze of delirium, his throat so filled with membrane that he felt choked and had to fight for breath, he found his father's sister Augusta seated beside his bed. Aunt Augusta told him that Kurt's and Kara's souls had gone to heaven, that their bodies were buried in Holy Name Cemetery.

A high, eerie sound cut harshly into Karl's fog-filled head; Aunt Augusta whispered that the sound was Maggie Rose, screaming. It went on endlessly until Karl heard his father shouting (his father, who never shouted), "They were my children, too! Do you think you're the only one who feels grief?"

His mother's screams had stopped then, but for months afterward her eyes were wild and hollow. Not until Henry was born did she smile again, and her smile had been unused for so long it looked ghostly.

After her children died, Maggie Rose hated both God and the Culleys. The dirty, poorly fed Culley children had somehow survived the diphtheria they gave to the Kerners, the diphtheria that killed two of Maggie Rose's clean, well-nourished, fiercely loved children. But because hatred of God was unnatural in Catholic-born-and-bred Maggie Rose, after a while she hated only the Culleys.

"What were their names again?" Henry asked.

"Kurt and Kara. See, Henry, when Mom and Pop started having children, they decided to give all of us names beginning with K, to go with Kerner. The boys had German first names and Irish middle names—Karl Patrick, and Kurt Brendan. The girls had it the other way around, Irish first names and German middle names—Kathleen Hilda and Kara Augusta."

"What's my middle name?"

"You don't have one," Karl answered. "After Kurt and Kara died, Mom broke the pattern. No more Ks. They named you Henry, without any middle name at all."

"Then my first name will be Henry and my middle name will be Hunnie," he said.

"That's a good idea," Karl told him. "Listen, promise you won't let Mom know that I've told you about Kurt and Kara. It would only make her sad." Just telling Henry about them had made Karl ache inside again. He still wept about Kurt and Kara sometimes at night, when he'd waken from a dream in which they were alive and happy and playing with him.

"I promise," Henry said.

"And promise me one more thing. Don't tell Mom that I spanked you."

Reminded of it, Henry began to whimper again. "My bum still hurts," he cried.

Karl hugged him. "I'm sorry. Promise me. Please?"

"If I promise," Henry said, "you have to buy me a present."

"I can't, Hun . . . Henry. I don't have any money."

"Then take me to see the fish."

Karl considered. Charles Bonner was no doubt still riding somewhere in his automobile. Karl could probably sneak Henry through the hedge, give him a quick look at the goldfish, and get him back home in time to feed him and put him to bed. Hoping the red handmarks on Henry's round bottom would fade before morning, before Maggie Rose could see them, Karl pulled up his little brother's pants and buttoned them.

When they reached the general superintendent's estate, Henry scooted through the hedge and ran toward the fishpond. Karl knelt to follow him, surprised to find that the branches of the hedge had been pushed aside with apparent force, making the opening wider than it had been an hour earlier. Inside the grounds, he looked around cautiously, but once again, the groundskeeper was nowhere in sight.

A movement caught his eye, though, from inside the ivy-covered gazebo that stood thirty feet farther along the hedge, surrounded by broad-leafed sycamore trees. Forgetting Henry for the moment, Karl crept silently toward the gazebo, curious to see who could be in it. He kept himself in the shade of the tall hedge until he could see through the gazebo's arched opening.

Inside it, Jame and Kathleen sat close together, talking too softly for Karl to hear their words. It was the wide yellow bow in the back of Kathleen's hair that had caught Karl's attention.

Kathleen, tall and well built, was a fine broth of a girl, their mother often said, but beside Jame she appeared dainty. His thick arm circled her shoulders; her dark curls spilled over his white shirtsleeve. Jame bent his head and Kathleen raised hers. They kissed for a long time.

Watching them, Karl felt heat and excitement stir inside his body, as though *he* were the one who was kissing a girl. Was that what it would feel like to be in love?—the hot rush of blood, and a feeling that was intensely pleasant but at the same time unbearably stimulating. Like being tickled when he was little, when he couldn't help laughing but at the same time was frantic to have it stop, because the pain/pleasure felt so savage.

Karl crept away from the gazebo. Kathleen and Jame never noticed him.

CHAPTER THREE

FORGING

1

School began, as always, on the day after Labor Day. At a quarter before nine Karl waited, along with nine other fellows and seventeen girls of the sophomore class of Canaan High School, for the arrival of the homeroom teacher, Professor Whiteside.

Resigned to the fate of attending school, Karl made the best of things by studying the sophomore girls, one by one, to see whether any of them had improved over the summer. He couldn't notice much difference, except that three of the girls, Tilly Horner, Esther Berkowitz, and Virginia Ward, had swept up their hair into grown-up styles, and wore ankle-length skirts. They were clustered in a corner with a few other girls singing softly:

> Ev'rybody's doin' it, doin' it, doin' it,
> See that ragtime couple over there,
> Watch them throw their shoulders in the air . . .

The singing stopped abruptly when a woman appeared in the doorway.

The woman walked quickly to the teacher's desk, turned to face them, and smiled. Instantly the room became silent. Not a foot shuffled, not a chair squeaked, and Virginia Ward halted in mid-giggle. The woman facing them was young, and beautiful in an unusual, arresting way.

"Young ladies and gentlemen," she said, "Professor White-side became ill this summer, and has gone to live with his daughter in West Virginia. I will be your new homeroom teacher. I will teach you grammar and English literature, as Professor Whiteside would have done. My name is Miss Petrov. Yulyona Petrov."

At the sound of the name, a subdued gasp filled the room. The woman swept to the blackboard and wrote in large capital letters: YULYONA PETROV.

She smiled at them again, a smile slightly off-center so that the left corner of her mouth rose a bit higher than the right, and her lower lip curved more fully on the right side. Though the smile was uneven, Karl thought it looked nice. Better than nice. Very pretty.

"I want to learn all your names as quickly as possible," Miss Petrov told them. "To make it easier for me, please choose the desks where you'd like to sit for the rest of the year. Choose them now."

Karl barely had time to untangle his long legs from around the wrought-iron legs of the desk he'd been sitting at. He scrambled to claim the desk closest to the teacher's, but Frank Platt and Eugene McNeary had reached it ahead of him. While they stood in the aisle arguing over the front center desk, Karl slipped into its seat.

"Gentlemen!" Miss Petrov sounded a bit startled. "We have thirty-six desks and twenty-seven pupils. Surely each of you can find a satisfactory place to sit." Frank and Eugene glared at each other, and both of them glared at Karl before they settled for seats in the second row.

"Very good. Now I will pass paper and pencils. You will write your name in large letters on the paper, and place it on your desk turned toward me so that I can see who you are. Young lady, will you kindly pass these pencils? You are . . . ?"

"Tilly Horner."

"Thank you, Tilly. And young man, would you pass the papers? Your name is . . . ?"

"Karl Kerner." He leaped to his feet, grabbing for the papers so quickly that the edge of one tore. "I'm sorry, Miss . . . "

"Never mind, it's only paper. Pass them, please. Since I want us to become acquainted, I'll begin by telling you something about myself. I was born in Russia, but came with my parents to America when I was four years old. My father is the cantor of the Russian Orthodox Church here in Canaan. Last June I received a degree in English literature from the University of Pittsburgh. I am twenty-four years old."

This time the class was too astonished to even gasp. Twenty-seven wide-eyed stares riveted Miss Petrov. Never in their nine previous years of school had the pupils heard a teacher discuss anything as personal as her *age!*

"Now tell me about yourselves," she said. "First, how many of you have reached your sixteenth birthdays?"

The three girls in long skirts raised their hands.

"None of you gentlemen?" Miss Petrov asked.

They shook their heads. The boys from their last-year's class who'd turned sixteen had already gone to work in the mills. Some had left even earlier, after eighth grade, to take the boy jobs in the steelworks.

Miss Petrov frowned, causing a thin line to appear between her full brown eyebrows. Then she said, "If I should ask you to stand up, one by one, and tell me about yourselves—which I would very much like to do—we might run out of time before Professor Dowling comes to teach you algebra. So, instead, turn over your papers and write something that will let me know who you are."

The pupils exchanged uncertain looks. No teacher had ever before wanted to know who they were. Tilly Horner hesitantly raised her hand to ask, "What should we write?"

Miss Petrov replied, "At the top of the paper, write your date of birth, including the year. Then . . . oh . . . tell me about your family, the kind of work you would like to do when you leave school, your favorite pastimes, your favorite books, just anything that will let me learn about the human being who occupies your seat."

Tilly Horner bit the tip of her pencil, not quite sure what that last part meant. Karl leaned sideways to watch Fred Hollingsted write in bold letters. "My birth date—February 6, 1897. I am an honor student."

Karl printed his own birth date—November 20, 1896. On the next line he wrote, "I have an older sister and a little brother. I like music. I never took piano lessons, but I can play by ear." He raised his pencil and rested his chin on his fist, wondering what else he could write about himself, something that would impress this new teacher.

His desk was just a little to the side of Miss Petrov's, and watching her he forgot to think about what he should write on the paper. Miss Petrov's head was bent over an open book, but she glanced up often to look at her students. On one of the glances Karl noticed her eyes—they were either light brown or gray, he wasn't certain, but he studied them until he decided that the color was a mixture of both brown and gray. Her eyes tilted slightly upward at the outer edges, and were rimmed by dark, curved lashes, over cheekbones higher than ordinary. She wore her hair swept up, caught in a coil so thick it would have filled both Karl's hands. The brown hair swelled in full curves from her temples to her crown, and the hairline was edged by fine tendrils that shone dull gold in the light from the windows. Gradually drifting into a daydream, Karl wondered how the fine gold tendrils would feel if he should reach out and touch them, curl them around his fingers.

Miss Petrov's eyes caught his and he flushed, dropping his gaze to the yellow paper on his desk. "Sometimes I make up songs," he wrote. That might impress her. Yulyona would be a wonderful name to build a song around, but the only word he could think of to rhyme with it was "dona." At Mass the priest said, "Dona nobis pacem." Give us peace.

All too soon Professor Dowling entered the room to teach algebra. Miss Petrov collected the students' papers and went to another room—would she want to know all about the freshmen, too, and the juniors and seniors she would teach this year? Karl groaned when Mr. Dowling passed out the algebra books, and Mr. Dowling shot him an angry glance. Karl had forgotten that from the front row, his every sound would be audible to the teacher, his every move visible. Still, it was worth it. After lunch, Miss Petrov would come back to teach literature.

Kathleen was waiting to walk home with him at lunchtime. Since they had to walk a mile and a half to their house, eat, walk a mile and a half back to school, and have it all done in the space of an hour and ten minutes, they moved quickly. The sun was hot overhead. Karl felt his underarms grow damp as he hurried across the vacant lots they cut through to save time. At home, he'd have to sprinkle talcum powder under his arms so he wouldn't smell disagreeable all afternoon, seated as close as he'd be to Miss Petrov.

"What did you think of Miss Petrov?" Kathleen asked, as though she'd read Karl's mind. "Isn't she peaches and creamy? It's so nice to have a young, pretty teacher for a change. The kids all liked her, even though she's kind of . . . different . . . in some ways. It's a good thing they do, because the teachers are going to give her trouble."

"What kind of trouble?" Karl asked.

"Oh, I was in the principal's office this morning before school started, getting some pencils for Professor Dowling, and I heard Miss Croft and Mr. Barney talking about her. They didn't know I was there, or else they wouldn't have said what they did."

Kathleen paused, waiting for a reaction from Karl.

"Well, go on. What did they say?"

"Miss Croft said, 'How did a hun . . .' I could tell she was going to say 'hunky,' Karl, but she caught herself and changed it to 'foreigner.' 'How did a foreigner ever get a job teaching in Canaan High School?'"

Karl was indignant. "That skinny, crabby old maid! Miss Croft's just jealous because she's wrinkled up like a walnut kernel, and Miss Petrov's . . ."

"Miss Petrov's what?" Kathleen asked.

"Like you said. Peaches and creamy. So what did Mr. Barney answer?"

"He said it was a disgrace, and what was Canaan School District coming to if they allowed people like Miss Petrov to teach, a woman who hadn't even been born in America, and was probably an anarchist."

"What's an anarchist?" Karl asked.

"Beats me! Whatever it is, Mr. Barney made it sound nasty."

"Shoot, he makes everything sound nasty," Karl said. "Do you think the teachers will really give her trouble?"

"Oh, they probably won't do anything mean to her, but it wouldn't surprise me a bit if they snub her today when the teachers eat lunch together."

Karl wished there were some way he could make it up to Miss Petrov if the teachers did snub her. "Say, Kathleen," he asked, "do you think Miss Petrov would like it if I took her some of Mom's zinnias after lunch?"

"I think she'd be real tickled," Kathleen answered.

Karl walked faster, mentally listing all the things he'd have to do while he was home for lunch: eat, use the talcum powder, pick zinnias, and wash the soot off them under the kitchen faucet. "Hurry up, Kathleen," he said.

"Wait, you're making me get out of breath. Anyway, there's something else I want to talk to you about, Karl."

"What?"

Kathleen smoothed her hair; heat and exertion had curled the fine hairs around her forehead into tight ringlets. "I just want to thank you ... about Jame. It's been really nice of you to pretend to walk me home from the nickelodeon this week, and let Jame do it instead."

Frowning, Karl said, "To tell you the truth, it doesn't make me feel very good to be putting one over on Mom like that." He glanced at her when he said that, and noticed her cheeks redden.

"Don't think I like it either," Kathleen told him. She sounded defensive. "But Mom's so darned unreasonable about the Culleys."

Karl asked, "Does it mean that much to you, just to have Jame walk you home? Is it worth it, bluffing Mom?"

"Listen, brother dear, I'm almost seventeen," Kathleen answered, "old enough to pick my own friends. Jame and I are just good friends, that's all."

Good friends! Karl wanted to exclaim. If you kiss all your friends the way I saw you kissing Jame, it's a wonder they aren't lined up all the way down Pine Alley to Center Street.

With a smile that seemed forced, Kathleen asked him, "What have you been doing with yourself between eight-thirty and nine-thirty for the past week?"

"Hanging around the billiards room inside the library. Sometimes, if I know a couple of the guys that are there, I shoot a game with them."

"As long as you're in the library, you ought to read a book once in a while," Kathleen told him.

Karl grimaced. "Reading's no fun, not for me. Andy likes to read, though. Did you know he's read almost every book in the . . . "

"You told me." They'd arrived at their back gate. Kathleen put her hand over Karl's as he reached to open it. "Anyway, thanks for what you're doing. And please be careful that Mom doesn't find out."

Karl had hurried ahead of Kathleen, hoping to be the first person back in the sophomore room after lunch, but when he got there, Frank Platt and Fred Hollingsted were already in their seats, and Eugene McNeary came through the door right behind him.

He'd mentally rehearsed the way he would present the zinnias, with a debonair smile and a slight bow, which would look gentlemanly but not sissy. With those three fellows watching him, though, he felt too conspicuous to do anything except thrust the flowers into Miss Petrov's hand and say, "Here!"

"Thank you!" She seemed genuinely pleased. When she smiled up at him, her lashes shadowed the high curve of her cheeks. "You're Karl Kerner, aren't you? I stayed in the classroom to eat lunch so that I'd have a chance to read all the papers. I was quite interested in yours, Karl. Would you mind remaining after school? I'd like to suggest something to you."

"Sure," he said, adding "Miss Petrov" when he realized how low-brow "Sure" sounded. He became aware of a sweet scent rising toward him. It wasn't the zinnias—he'd carried the zinnias all the way from home and he knew their pungent smell. The fragrance was much nicer, like violets, and it came from Miss Petrov herself. Karl breathed deeply, then backed away from her desk when Miss Petrov looked inquiringly at him.

At exactly one o'clock Miss Petrov stood up in front of the class. "Young ladies and gentlemen," she began, "we're going to start our study of English literature with the Shakespearean sonnets. They are poems about love."

A low rustle filled the room at the word *love*, a blend of seat twitchings, foot shufflings, whispers, and suppressed sighs, which indicated that the sophomores found the topic beguiling.

"The Shakespearean sonnets," Miss Petrov continued, "aren't only about the joy of love freely given and accepted, they're also about the pain of love rejected. But before we begin to read the first sonnet in our book, I'll tell you something about the life of William Shakespeare."

Miss Petrov's voice was full enough to be heard throughout the classroom, yet so soothing that Karl's mind began to wander. The inside air felt hot and still. A fly buzzed against a windowpane, droning in a monotonous hum. As she talked, Miss Petrov moved slowly and gracefully across the front of the room, never very far from Karl. Her beauty settled softly over his dreaming, like a pleasant mist; he pillowed his cheeks on his palms and let the mist envelop him. When he noticed a sheen of perspiration on her upper lip, he unconsciously licked his own lip, tasting salt.

The door banged open when Miss Croft arrived to teach penmanship. Karl jerked awake, frowning irritably at Miss Croft. During the rest of the afternoon, he drowned in boredom while teachers who seemed old and drab in contrast to Miss Petrov taught penmanship, elocution, and American history. He longed for the final bell, eager and a little nervous because Miss Petrov wanted him to stay after school.

Five minutes after the bell sounded, Miss Petrov returned to the classroom, which was empty except for Karl. For an instant she seemed surprised to see him, but then she said, "Oh yes, Karl Kerner. I asked you to remain, didn't I?"

He nodded, hurt that she'd forgotten the meeting he'd

anticipated for two hours and forty-three minutes by the dragging classroom clock.

"Sit for a minute, Karl," she told him, "while I find the book I'm looking for. Here it is. It occurred to me, when I read the paper you wrote . . . first, let me ask you. Had you ever read any of the Shakespearean sonnets before today?"

"No, ma'am."

"Well, it doesn't matter. On your paper, you wrote that you sometimes make up songs. I thought you might enjoy choosing one of the sonnets and setting it to music. They were originally sung, you know—the ones first written by medieval poets. If you'd like to give it a try, I'll lend you my book of Shakespearean sonnets, which has all of them in it. You can pick whichever one you like and write music for it."

She looked at him with such expectation that he dreaded what he had to tell her. "Miss Petrov, I don't know how to write down music."

"You don't?"

"No, ma'am. I can make up songs in my head, and I can pick out the tunes on the piano, but I can't read music or write the notes like in sheet music."

"I see."

To try to make amends for the disappointment he felt he must be causing her, Karl suggested, "I could write it down in do re mi fa sol, though. Would that be all right?"

"Of course, Karl. Any way you wish. And there's no hurry— just turn it in before the end of the first report card period. I'd like you to return the book just as soon as you've picked out a sonnet and copied it, though. The book doesn't belong to the school, it belongs to me, and it's very precious to me."

After he'd left the school and reached the street, Karl raised the front cover of the book to look inside. On the title page, beneath the printed words "The Complete Book of Shakespearean Sonnets," was the handwritten inscription: *For Yulyona Petrova, from her loving brother, Aleksei, January 7, 1908.*

3

It didn't take the sophomores long to learn how easy it was to distract Miss Petrov from teaching grammar. If someone asked a thoughtful question in the first half hour, Miss Petrov could be counted on to forget the lesson and talk on and on until Professor Dowling arrived to teach algebra.

By the end of the first week they found out why she wanted to know their birth dates. Her primary mission, she explained, was to persuade them to stay in high school until they graduated, rather than to leave school the day they turned sixteen.

"Nothing benefits a person more than education," she told them. "It took me seven years to earn my degree from the University of Pittsburgh, because I often had to stop attending classes to earn money for tuition. But I was determined to graduate, and it was worth the wait and the work."

"How did you earn the money?" Esther Berkowitz asked.

"By taking whatever jobs I could get. I worked in a glass factory, etching designs on lamp chimneys. Once I sewed feathers on ladies' hats. Another time I bottled pickles in the Heinz plant in Pittsburgh."

"Gee whiz," Virginia Ward said. "I'd hate to bottle pickles." Miss Petrov smiled wryly. "I doubt that you'll ever have to, Virginia, especially since your father will probably become state senator from Canaan in the next few years."

A thoughtful look narrowed Miss Petrov's eyes, made them

seem even more slanted. "Canaan," she said. "It's ironic that this town is called Canaan. Do any of you know where the name Canaan comes from?"

"I do," Fred said, waving his hand. "It's from the Bible. The people of ancient Canaan were heathens who didn't believe in the one true God."

"That's correct, Fred. The people of ancient Canaan worshiped the false god Baal. They sacrificed little children by throwing them into the fires of Baal, where the children were burned to death." Miss Petrov placed her hands on Karl's desk and leaned forward. Her expression grew intense, as it often did when she was trying to impress her students with an important thought.

"Here, in Canaan, Pennsylvania, we have a practice that is just as horrible as the child sacrifice of ancient Canaan," she said. "Boys like you . . . ," she looked at each one in turn, " . . . when you reach your sixteenth birthdays, leave school to work in the Canaan steel mills. Just as the people of ancient Canaan sacrificed their children to the fire-god Baal, the people of Canaan, Pennsylvania, sacrifice their sons to the fires of the blast furnaces."

"That's not true," Karl said quietly. "Our parents don't make us go into the mills. We go because we want to."

Miss Petrov stared at Karl. Her brown-gray eyes seemed to fill with pain. "I know," she whispered, "and that makes it all the more tragic."

She lowered her head and gripped the edges of Karl's desk until her knuckles whitened, as though she were wrestling with some private grief. The tension in the classroom mounted as the students watched her, wondering what was hurting her. Finally Eugene McNeary raised his hand to ask,

"What's wrong with working in the mill, Miss Petrov? Nearly all the men in Canaan do."

"Men, Eugene," she said, and although her voice wavered, she was in control again. "The mill jobs should be limited to men, grown men, not boys like you. Even for grown men, the work is dangerous. How many of you know a man who lost an arm or leg in the mill, or was badly burned, or even . . . killed?"

Every hand went up.

"You see? That's why I want you to stay in school, to get your high school diplomas, at least. Then perhaps you can become further educated to do some other kind of work, rather than risking your lives in the steel mills as though there were no alternative."

Karl closed his grammar book and leaned back in his seat. Miss Petrov was the most beautiful, intelligent, and exciting woman he'd ever known, but she talked foolishness. What else was there for a man to do in Canaan, P.A., except go into the mills?

4

Andrew Carnegie had intended all his free public libraries to become community centers, and had equipped the one in Canaan with an indoor swimming pool, an auditorium, showers for people who didn't have plumbing in their homes, and a billiards room to keep the young men off the streets, all in addition to the books.

During the first week that Karl had deceived his mother by pretending to go after Kathleen at the nickelodeon, he'd hung around the library's billiards room each evening between 8:45 and 9:15, for lack of anything better to do. After

Miss Petrov gave him the book of Shakespearean sonnets, he'd begun spending those half hours in the library's reading room, paging through the book with a despair that grew deeper each night.

He'd never much liked reading, anyway, and the sonnets were moldy, unintelligible bunk. How could anyone make up a tune for lines like, "And heavily from woe to woe tell o'er the sad account of fore-bemoaned moan," or "More than that tongue that more hath more expressed."

After twelve evenings spent raking through the mire of verses that made no sense, Karl decided to tell Miss Petrov that he couldn't do it, that the job was too much for him. He'd stay after school the following afternoon, a Tuesday, and explain it to her. She might be disappointed, but she'd have to accept the fact that Karl wasn't an honor student like Fred.

By that time they'd gone past the Shakespearean sonnets in class and were reading *Antony and Cleopatra,* which was as bad as the sonnets. That Tuesday, after lunch, Miss Petrov called on Karl to read aloud. He stayed seated at his desk, as she'd told the students to do when they were reciting only a few lines.

"I found you as a morsel cold upon dead Caesar's trencher," Karl began. "Nay, you were a fragment of . . . "

He stopped reading. How in the world was the next word—*Gneius*—pronounced?

Miss Petrov came to stand beside his desk, asking, "What is it you're having trouble with, Karl? Point out the line to me."

He had his finger on the word, and raised his head toward her just as she leaned over his desk. By accident, the edge of his lips brushed the curve of her breast, that full, firm breast covered by thin lavender cloth that smelled of violets.

Jerking backward as though he'd been stung, Karl lowered his head so that his face hung only inches above the open book.

"Gneius." She pronounced it for him as if nothing had happened. "Continue reading, Karl. '. . . of Gneius Pompey's; besides what hotter hours . . . '"

The words swam before his eyes, swam, then congealed, then flew apart so that he couldn't recognize a single letter, let alone a whole word. "Gneius," he croaked, not because he could read it, but because he'd heard her say it.

"Never mind," she told him softly, and her voice, so close, dizzied his head the way her presence electrified his body.

"Eugene, would you begin reading from 'besides what hotter hours . . . '?" she asked, moving away from Karl's desk, leaving him drenched with confusion and perspiration.

He couldn't stay after school that afternoon because he was still too shaken by the chance contact with such an unthinkable part of Miss Petrov; each time he did think of it, his lips burned. That evening in the library, he sat with her book before him, softly brushing his fingers over her name in the inscription. Yulyona Petrova. Yulyona.

He let the pages fall open at a place of their own choosing, and the sonnet appeared uncannily before his eyes:

> Being your slave, what should I do but tend
> Upon the hours and times of your desire?
> I have no precious time at all to spend,
> Nor services to do, till you require.

Perfect. Before he'd copied the first quatrain, the melody was in his head.

He was whistling it when he met Kathleen and Jame on

the dip below the middle dip of Center Street. After they said good night to Jame, who stayed in the shadows outside the periphery of the streetlight's illumination, Karl whistled it again as he and Kathleen climbed the last half of Center Street toward Pine Alley.

"That's pretty," she told him. "Did you make it up?"

"Um hmmm." He would return the book to Miss Petrov the next day, but it would take him a while to gather enough courage to sing the sonnet for her.

Kathleen said, "I've been thinking, Karl. You're so musical, I want to teach you some of the songs I play at the nickelodeon."

"Why?"

"Well, if ever I get . . . sick, or something, you could fill in for me. The songs aren't hard; you could just play the melody with one hand and chord with the other. You have to watch the screen while you're playing the piano, though, so you'll be sure to get the right kind of music with the different scenes. Like in the sad scenes I play 'Hearts and Flowers,' and when the cavalry rides in, I play the William Tell Overture. You know, da-da-dum, da-da-dum, da-da-dum-dum-dum."

"Would the theater manager let me fill in for you?" Karl asked.

"Why not? He has a tin ear and can't tell one song from another, so if you made any mistakes, he wouldn't even know it. Would you do it for me—learn the songs? You can keep the fifty cents a night, if it ever happens that I can't play for one reason or another."

"Sure," Karl said, "if you think I can play well enough."

"Don't worry about that. I'll start teaching you after school tomorrow. You have such a good ear, you'll learn fast."

On the fourth Sunday after Karl had seen Kathleen and Jame kissing in the gazebo, Maggie Rose and Hugo Kerner didn't go to Pittsburgh. They stayed at home to entertain Hugo's euchre club.

By seven in the evening, the nine men had arrived, filling the kitchen with the smell of perspiration and cigar smoke. Because it was a hot evening toward the end of September, they'd begun to remove the high, starched collars from their shirts soon after they greeted Maggie Rose. Once they were seated around the kitchen table, they unbuttoned their cuffs, too, and rolled their shirtsleeves to their elbows.

Since the kitchen was double the size of any other room in the Kerner house, the card parties always took place there. Karl leaned against the doorframe to watch Tommie Digman shuffle the cards as the other men settled their bulk into the wooden chairs.

"Tonight we're not going to play for money," Karl's father announced.

"What?" Ambrose Olbein asked, only he pronounced it "Vass?" because his German accent was still thick.

"I said we'll not play for money tonight," Hugo repeated.

"You're joshing us, eh, Hugo?" Tommie Digman asked.

"I mean it, Tommie," Hugo told him. "Didn't you read the newspaper? Last week Mayor Ward announced that all gambling was illegal in Canaan from now on. *All* gambling. I respect the law. If no gambling is allowed in the borough of Canaan, I will not allow gambling in my house."

Maggie Rose returned the ham she'd been slicing to the

icebox, looking over at Hugo as if she thought he was behaving foolishly.

"Ve only play for pennies . . . ," Ambrose Olbein began, and Jack Kratzer interrupted with, "What fun is it to play cards without an ante?"

"We can play euchre as usual," Hugo insisted. "We just won't play for pennies."

All the men grumbled, and one of them argued, "Mayor Ward was just talking about gambling in the saloons and hotels, Hugo. He didn't mean in people's houses."

"Hold on a moment, chaps," Tommie Digman broke in. "Hugo respects the law, and I respect Hugo. If he doesn't want us to play for pennies in his house, then perhaps we can play for matchsticks. After the game's over, you chaps can settle up in the alley. How does that strike you, Hugo?"

"Like a match." Hugo smiled, and a few of the players who weren't too disgruntled chuckled at the pun. Looking around for Karl, Hugo called, "Son, run down to Santori's and get four boxes of wooden matches. Go quick like a rabbit."

From the corner of the kitchen where she was fixing food for the euchre players, Maggie Rose pursed her lips and shook her head over her husband's rigid code of honor. "As long as you're going to the grocer's," she told Karl, "bring back a box of soda crackers."

By the time Karl returned from the grocery store, the euchre club members were in better spirits. The bung had been tapped on the half keg of beer, and a foam-topped stein sat before each of the men, who had started to play with as many matches as Maggie Rose could find in the house. When Karl handed the four boxes to his father, Hugo divided the extra matches into ten piles.

Shortly after the game had begun in earnest, Maggie Rose stared out through the kitchen window and remarked, "Mother of God, Mayo Culley's coming through our backyard heading for the door. What does the likes of him want at this house?"

Hugo started to say, "Now, Maggie, . . . " but she added, "There's a man with him."

Karl had already gone to the door to open it for Jame's father, Mayo Culley. Slightly behind Mayo stood a good-looking, florid-faced man wearing a tailor-made pin-striped suit and a necktie pierced with a pearl stickpin.

"Ah, good evenin' to ye, Karl," Mayo Culley said. "If memory serves me right, this is the night of your father's euchre club get-together, is it not? I brought the honorable mayor, Harry Ward, over here to do a little politickin' amongst the card-players."

Hugo had risen to invite the men inside. "Come in, Harry, come in," he said. "Haven't seen you for a while. Come in, Mayo."

Maggie Rose deliberately avoided Mayo Culley's eyes as Hugo introduced first her, then the euchre club members, to Mayor Ward.

"Don't let me interrupt your game, boys," Harry Ward said, glancing toward the cards on the table. "I just came to have a few words with you fellows about the election coming up. From the looks of you, I'm sure you're all registered Republicans, since I can see that you're all men of good sense." He smiled, showing small, even teeth.

"Interrupt the game all you want," Jack Kratzer grumbled. "It sure ain't much of a game with matchsticks. Hugo won't let us play for pennies because of that ban on gambling you put in last week's *Canaan Times*."

"Is that a fact?" Ward asked.

"We told Hugo you only meant no gambling in saloons and public houses," Tommie Digman said, "but Hugo's determined to be more honest than the president of the United States."

"That ain't so honest," Jack Kratzer joked, and all the men laughed.

Harry Ward frowned. He didn't like anyone to joke about William Howard Taft, who had the backing of the steel corporation in his bid for reelection to the presidency. "If you vote for Taft in November," Ward told them, "you'll be keeping an honest man in the White House, and the steel mills will do better than ever. What's good for the steel mills is good for the borough of Canaan; just remember that when it's time to vote."

Glancing around at them, Ward cleared his throat. "As for the government of Canaan, I personally guarantee you men that I'm cleaning out any corruption I find in any of the departments. Just yesterday I fired the chief of police because I learned he was taking graft. The very minute I found out about it, I kicked him out."

"Ye fired the chief of the police, did I hear ye say?" Mayo Culley asked.

"That's what I just said. I fired him yesterday."

"And you'll be appointin' a new one, is it?"

"That's right, Mayo. A decent, honest man . . . as soon as I can find one somewhere," Ward said, making the cardplayers laugh again.

"Well, the Lord himself couldn't come up with a more decent man than Hugo Kerner here," Mayo declared. "You'd be doin' all of Canaan a favor if you'd appoint Hugo chief of the police."

Hugo's mouth opened in astonishment. Harry Ward squinted toward Hugo. Karl looked from one man to the other, growing excited.

"I'm tellin' you," Mayo went on, "in all of Canaan you'd not find another man who would forbid gambling in his own home just on account of some lines in a newspaper. On the wild coast of County Mayo where I grew up, there was decent men aplenty, but never a one more decent than Hugo here. That's the God's truth."

The euchre club members began to agree out loud with Mayo Culley, even the ones who'd objected to playing euchre without pennies. Harry Ward ran a finger over his jaw as he studied Hugo with still-narrowed eyes.

"How 'bout it, Hugo?" Ward asked softly. "Would you like to be chief of police for the borough of Canaan?"

"I ... my job in the mill ...," Hugo stammered.

"Don't let that stop you," Ward told him. "I'm on friendly terms with superintendent Charles Bonner. He wants honest government in this town too. You could start as police chief in a couple of days, if you want to. Bonner will make everything right with your foreman."

Hugo asked, "Wouldn't it be kind of ... peculiar ... to pluck someone like me out of the mill and make him police chief? I don't know anything about police work."

"No problem, no problem at all," Ward answered with a wave of his hand. "In Canaan, the chief of police is mostly a ... a figurehead, if you know what I mean. To be perfectly honest, Kerner, the job is a political plum, and the appointment is left entirely up to me. Just now I need someone of unimpeachable honesty to show the voters that I'm running a clean town."

Still hesitant, Hugo inquired, "What would the work be?"

"You won't have to go out and pound a beat or anything like that, Hugo. You'll just make up the schedules for the officers, escort prisoners when they have to be extradited to another town, and read aloud the department reports at city council meetings once in a while," Ward told him. "As for salary . . . how much do you make in the mill?"

"Twenty-three dollars a week."

"Then how 'bout twenty-five a week as police chief? You can use the extra to take the little woman out in the evenings every now and then, since you won't have to work night turns. What do you say, Hugo?"

"Maggie Rose?" Hugo asked, looking to her to help him decide.

"Whatever you want is fine with me, Hugo," she told him.

Karl wanted to shout his encouragement—he'd be so proud to have his father become chief of police—but he knew he mustn't break into the conversation between his father and Mayor Ward. Instead, he bounded up the stairs to find Kathleen, who was lying on her bed reading a story to Henry, enjoying her Sunday night off from the nickelodeon.

"Kathleen, come downstairs quick," he cried softly. "You'll never guess what's happening. Pop might be chief of police."

"What! You're kidding!"

"No. Harry Ward's down in the kitchen right now talking to Pop about it."

"I want to come too," Henry said, scrambling off the bed.

The three of them clattered down the steps and reached the kitchen just as Harry Ward shook their father's hand. "Be at city hall at eight in the morning, Hugo," Ward was saying, "and I'll swear you into office."

"Won't the borough council have to approve me first?" Hugo asked.

"Don't worry about the council. They'll do whatever I . . . that is, they'll agree that you're the right man for the job."

After Harry Ward had left, the kitchen erupted into a happy tumult. The cardplayers jumped up to shake Hugo's hand or pound him on the back. Kathleen kissed her father and Karl hugged Henry, who didn't understand what all the excitement was about but hugged Karl back anyway.

Over the hubbub Mayo Culley's voice rang out. "God increase you, Hugo! And to think this all came about on account of Harry Ward stopped by my house this night. He'd heard our Jame was out of work, and he came to ask if Jame wanted to earn a bit of cash tackin' up Taft posters all over town."

Mayo seemed to puff with importance as the men quieted to hear him. "Then Harry Ward started askin' me how I was goin' to vote," Mayo said, "and I told him if he wanted to do some politickin' there was a gang of voters over here at this house. And if that didn't lead to Hugo becomin' chief of the police. God in Glory, this calls for a celebration!"

"Get Mayo a glass of beer, Karl," Hugo said, smiling broadly.

"To hell with the euchre game," Jack Kratzer yelled. "Let's drink to Police Chief Hugo Kerner!"

Smiling even wider, Hugo said, "Never mind, Karl, I'll get Mayo his beer. You go bring me my mouth organ."

The cards and match sticks were swept aside on the tabletop. Kathleen helped Maggie Rose carry platters of sliced ham, cheese, bread, pickles, crackers and hard-boiled eggs to set on the table as the men took turns at the keg, refilling their beer steins. Holding his glass in his left hand, because his right hand had been crippled years earlier in a mill accident, Mayo Culley drank all the beer in one long quaff, then lined up to refill at the keg.

When Hugo began to play a waltz on his harmonica, the boisterous men jumped to their feet to dance with one another, as they always did after the cardplaying ended at the Kerner house. Since most of them were middle-aged and had bellies that protruded almost as much as President William Howard Taft's, the force of their combined weights, as they stomped and whirled around the kitchen, made the floorboards sink and heave alarmingly.

"Here, Karl, you play," Hugo said, thrusting the harmonica into Karl's hands. "I'm going to dance with your mother."

Karl would rather have played the piano, but since the piano was in the parlor and would hardly be heard over the din in the kitchen, he began to blow on the harmonica. "Waltz Me Around Again, Willie," he played, and Henry climbed on a chair to sing, "Around and around and around."

Hugo bent to circle his arm around Maggie Rose's waist. Laughing up at him, she cried, "Let me take my apron off, for Lord's sake!"

Kathleen leaned against the wall, smiling as she watched her tall, broad father and her short, sturdy mother swoop among the couples of thick-paunched men. Then the skinniest, shortest man in the crowd strutted forward to ask Kathleen to dance.

"It's a grand night this is, Kathleen," Mayo Culley shouted above the noise. "Let you come out then to dance with me."

"I'd be honored, Mr. Culley." Standing half a head taller than Mayo Culley, Kathleen held out her arms and dipped a graceful curtsy. As they began to dance, Mayo kicked a few

Irish jig steps into the waltz, saying, "Me hand may be maimed, but there's nothin' wrong with these two feet."

"There certainly isn't," Kathleen agreed, laughing.

Maggie Rose was laughing, too, twirling in Hugo's arms until she caught sight of Kathleen with Mayo Culley. She stopped so abruptly that Hugo stumbled.

"Kathleen!" she cried, in a voice piercing enough to cut through the clamor in the kitchen like a bullet through glass.

Bright spots of color flamed in Kathleen's cheeks, but she ignored her mother and went on waltzing with Mayo. Some of the men had to stop dancing to keep from bumping into Maggie Rose, who stood rooted to the floor, her back as rigid as a steel rod.

"Kathleen!" Maggie Rose cried again.

When he saw what was happening, Karl's breath caught so that he couldn't play another note. The din in the kitchen dwindled to silence.

"Go to your room," Maggie Rose ordered her daughter.

"Maggie Rose, you will not make a scene," Hugo told his wife, his voice grim.

"Is it that I'm not good enough to dance with your daughter?" Mayo Culley asked in a rising tone. "And after meself gettin' your mister a fancy job with the police?"

"Of course you may dance with my daughter," Hugo said. "Play another song, Karl."

Karl looked uncertainly from his mother to his father, then began to play a German waltz. With a defiant look at her mother, Kathleen placed her hand on Mayo's crippled one.

Mayo slipped his arm around Kathleen's waist. Tossing his head and grinning at Hugo, Mayo said, "It's grand to see you keepin' your wife in line for a change, Hugo."

Fury surged into Maggie Rose's face. "Wait, stop the song, Karl," she cried. "Here's a better one for Mayo to dance to!" In her strident voice she sang:

> Everybody works but father,
> He sits around all day,
> Feet up by the fire,
> Smoking his pipe of clay.
> Mother takes in washing . . .

"Maggie Rose!" Hugo thundered. "That's enough!"

Mayo Culley's face had paled. "You've a score of devils inside you, Maggie Rose," he said. "You know full well I'd work if I had the use of two good hands." Moving away from Kathleen, Mayo declared in a loud voice, "It's here I'd liefer stay to celebrate the night with my friend Hugo, but I'll not remain in a house where I'm insulted by a woman."

With his chin raised as though that would compensate for his lack of height, Mayo Culley stalked across the kitchen. At the door he turned to face Maggie Rose. In spite of his shortness, his bowed legs, and his shabby clothes, he emanated dignity as he proclaimed, "Good night to all in this house. And may God forgive you, Maggie Rose."

Kathleen began to cry.

CHAPTER FOUR

WELDING

1

"Twenty, twenty-five, thirty, thirty-five." Andy finished stacking the nickels on the edge of his porch. "We have a dollar thirty-five to buy Veronica's wedding present."

Karl said, "We ought to be able to get something pretty nice for that. Got any ideas?"

"Nope. Do you?"

"She's your sister," Karl told Andy. "You ought to know what she'd like."

Andy pushed the stacks of nickels into a straight line, like lead soldiers. "Veronica already has all kinds of stuff put away," he said. "She and Mama have been stitching towels and cro-cheting doilies for the past couple of months."

"How about a pitcher and a wash basin?" Karl suggested.

"She's got that. Maybe you should just take a walk down street and look in the store windows to see if you can find something."

"Me? Why me?"

"'Cause I won't have time to," Andy answered. "Tomorrow night after work I have to go over to the Sokol Hall and help clean it up. Friday night I have to help set up benches and chairs, and Saturday's the wedding."

"We shouldn't have waited this long to buy a present," Karl muttered. It was the ninth of October; only three days were left until Veronica's wedding. Although the weather remained mild, darkness gathered earlier each evening, so that even though it was only a little past supper, the stack of nickels had become indistinct gray knobs on Andy's back porch.

"Don't get sore at me, Andy," Karl said, "but I'd feel silly picking out a wedding present all by myself. Anyway, I'd probably get the wrong thing. I never bought a wedding present before."

"I'm not sore at you." Andy scooped the nickels into a handkerchief and twisted the edges to make a sack. "Listen, I've got a better idea. If we could come up with sixty-five more cents between us, that would make two dollars. We could change the money into two one-dollar bills. That way each of us could have one for the bride's dance."

"Bride's dance?"

"Yeah. There's always a bride's dance at a Slovak wedding party," Andy said. "The musicians play a real long dance, and every man who can afford a dollar gets to take a turn dancing with the bride. At a big wedding they sometimes collect as much as fifty bucks for the bride and groom to buy furniture and stuff for their house. If you can put in thirty cents, I'll try to sneak the other thirty-five cents out of my pay on Friday."

"Sneak it out? Don't you get to keep any of your pay?" Karl asked.

Andy let out a short, derisive laugh. "I never get a cent.

My old man takes every penny of my pay. If I need anything, from a pencil to a pair of shoestrings, he doles out the cash to me, and does he ever gripe about it! But maybe this Friday he'll be too busy with the wedding to count my pay."

Karl felt sorry for Andy. Karl never had any cash of his own, but then he wasn't earning any money either, and when he needed to buy something, his parents gave him the money without complaint. "I can get the thirty cents easy enough," he said, "because tomorrow after school I'm supposed to shovel coal into the Kratzers' coal cellar. Jack Kratzer hurt his back, so Mrs. Kratzer asked me to do it. She said she'd pay me a quarter, and I can get the other nickel from my folks."

Karl was glad Mrs. Kratzer had offered him the job—it would give him an excuse to stay away from home for a couple of extra hours after school. If he took his time shoveling the coal down the Kratzers' coal chute, he wouldn't get home until after Kathleen had left for the nickelodeon.

The Kerner family had been ill at ease since the night Maggie Rose insulted Mayo Culley. Hugo and Maggie Rose had made up their quarrel quickly, as they always did, but Kathleen stayed aloof, speaking to her mother only in curt answers to Maggie Rose's questions. For three days Kathleen's resentment toward her mother had kept Karl on edge, waiting for Maggie Rose to lash out in hot-tongued rebuke, but Maggie Rose had kept her temper in check. From time to time she glanced guardedly toward Kathleen, almost as if she wanted to apologize. That would go against all Maggie Rose's inclinations, though. Mothers weren't supposed to apologize to their children. A mother is always right, Maggie Rose firmly believed. That's why God made mothers.

2

On the afternoon of the day Veronica Stulak married Emil Hrenko, Hugo Kerner had to transfer a prisoner from the Canaan jail to the Pittsburgh lockup. The prisoner had shot another man in the leg, in the heat of a barroom argument about the relative merits of Theodore Roosevelt and William Howard Taft, both of whom were running for the presidency. Following the shooting in a Pittsburgh saloon, the assailant hopped a streetcar bound for Canaan, P.A., in full view of dozens of witnesses. Hugo met the streetcar at the Canaan stop, arrested the fugitive, and escorted the man, who had in the meantime sobered into meekness, to the Canaan jail, prior to delivering him to Pittsburgh.

Extraditing prisoners was one of the few duties Harry Ward expected Hugo to perform. What Ward hadn't expected was Hugo's objection to the idle hours that came with his "figure-head" position. To get paid for doing next to nothing went against Hugo's grain. After two weeks of unproductive days, he'd begun to study the police department records, hoping to teach himself something about police business.

On that October 12, though, Hugo did have a prisoner to extradite, so he sent home a message that he'd have to miss the Stulak wedding reception. Since Maggie Rose didn't want to go without her husband, and Kathleen had to work at the nickelodeon, Karl was the only member of the Kerner family getting cleaned up at four in the afternoon.

Karl poured hot water from the kettle into the basin and set it on a shelf next to the kitchen sink. Studying his face in the mirror above the shelf, he lathered his father's shaving brush against the soap in his father's shaving mug, and applied the foam to a suggestion of dark fuzz on his upper lip. With great caution, Karl eased his father's straight razor along his lip, then washed his face, arms, and underarms before dumping the soapy water into the sink.

Upstairs in his room, Karl put on a white shirt so heavily starched that he had to force his hands through the stuck-together sleeves. After pushing the collar button in the front of the shirt through the tiny buttonholes of a stiff high collar, he stretched his neck to ease the chafing. The blue bow tie turned out right on his first attempt at tying it, which he took as an omen that he'd look classy when he finished dressing. Long, thin legs through the trousers of his one good suit, suspenders snapped into place, vest buttoned all the way up, jacket settled smoothly over his shoulders, one last sweep of a comb through his pompadour in front of his mother's dresser mirror, and he was ready. He looked at least seventeen, he thought.

Electricity had been wired throughout the Sokol Hall the year before. Strings of forty-watt light bulbs, supplied by the light company at an inflated price, glowed over the middle of the floor, but left in shadow the benches along the walls where most of the guests were sitting.

Karl stood against the far wall, feeling shy and out of place because every bit of conversation he could hear was in Slovak. Across the room, the bride and groom sat at a long table with Andy's mother and father, the groom's brother Vaclav, a priest, and other dressed-up people Karl supposed were members of the bridal party. Karl searched the dimly lighted hall for Andy, and spotted him at the same time Andy saw Karl.

"Hey, you made it!" Andy cried, grabbing Karl's arm. "Where's the rest of your family?"

"Pop had to work late, and Mom didn't want to come without him. Mom said to tell your folks she's sorry about not coming. Here, I brought Veronica's wedding present from my mom and pop. Where should I put it?"

"Over on this table by the door," Andy told him.

"It's a cut-glass candy dish," Karl said. "Did you get the dollar bills for you and me to dance with Veronica?"

"Yeah, they're in my pocket. The bride's dance won't be till later, though. Come on and get something to eat."

Andy led Karl to a table filled with pastries and cookies shaped in crescents, bows, and balls. "That's kiflic, that's chrusciki, buchta, paherai, kolachy," Andy said, pointing to one pastry after another, amusing himself by bombarding Karl with Slovak words. "Grab a handful. You'll need strength when the dancing starts."

"Dancing!" Karl drew back. "Andy, I don't know how to dance your kind of dances."

"Listen, Karl, by the time the dancing starts, everybody'll be feeling too high to notice if you make mistakes."

After loading Karl's hands with cookies, Andy guided him to one of the benches lining the walls. "Sit here. I'll sit with you."

As he ate the cookies, which were delicious, Karl watched the bridal table. Toasts were being shouted in Slovak and drunk with laughter and sly glances at the bride and groom, who had been married eight hours earlier at a Mass in Holy Trinity Church. Veronica blushed at the good-natured teasing; her husband, Emil, grinned sheepishly. Everyone grew sober, though, when the priest rose to lift his glass and pronounce,

"Za Boha a národ." All the men stood up and repeated with fervor, *"Za Boha a národ."*

"Get up," Andy whispered to Karl. Both of them stood while the men raised their glasses to their lips and tossed back the drinks.

"What were they saying?" Karl asked after they sat down again.

"For God and country," Andy answered, "and believe me, when those men say 'country' they mean America. Slovaks are probably the most patriotic people in the whole U.S.A. That's why it makes me so dang mad, Karl, when the mill bosses call us union agitators and anarchists."

Karl asked, "Andy, what's an anarchist? That's the second time I've heard the word, and I don't know what it means."

"It's someone who wants to overthrow the government by violence," Andy explained.

As if the word had conjured her, Yulyona Petrov drifted toward the bridal table. She spoke to Veronica, embraced her, and shook Emil's hand.

"That's my teacher, Miss Petrov," Karl whispered excitedly. "What's she doing here?"

"Yulyona? She and Veronica are good friends. They used to play together when they were little, before we moved to the house we live in now."

"Why didn't you tell me she was a friend of your family?" Karl asked accusingly. "I told you she was my teacher, way back when school first started."

Surprised, Andy answered, "I don't know why I didn't tell you. I didn't think it was important, I guess. What difference does it make?"

"It makes a lot of difference. You could've told me things about her."

"Like what? What do you want to know?"

"Just . . . things," Karl replied lamely.

Andy raised his eyebrows, and then, as though to humor Karl, began, "Well, she's about the same age as Veronica . . . ."

"She's twenty-four," Karl said.

"So she's a year older than Veronica. Anyway, her father is the cantor at the Russian Church."

"Russian Orthodox Church," Karl corrected.

"Yeah . . . well, her mother died . . . oh, maybe six years ago. Her brother died about three years ago."

"Her brother Aleksei?" Karl asked. He'd read the inscription in the book of sonnets: For Yulyona Petrova, from her loving brother, Aleksei.

"You know, for someone who's so anxious to hear everything about Yulyona, you seem to know plenty already," Andy remarked. "Yeah, Aleksei was her only brother. There were just the two kids in the Petrov family. Hey, do you want me to get you a bottle of pop to wash down the cookies?"

"No, stay here," Karl said, grabbing Andy's arm. "I want to hear more about Miss Petrov. How did her brother die?"

"In the mill. He was working on a platform near the top of C furnace when there was a slip. The whole top blew apart, and the explosion knocked Aleksei off the platform. He fell almost seventy feet to the ground. His skull was smashed."

"Ugh!" Karl swallowed to dislodge food which seemed stuck in his throat. "How old was Aleksei?"

"I don't know," Andy said. "Wait . . . yes, I do know. He'd just turned sixteen. He quit school on his sixteenth birthday to go to work in the mill, and he'd only been working three days when the slip blew him off the platform."

Karl couldn't eat the last chrusciki. He'd lost his appetite. He understood now why Miss Petrov was so intent on keeping her students in school. "How did she take it when her brother died?" he asked.

"Awful. She was crazy about Aleksei, kind of took over being his mother after their own mother died. So it really hit her hard. She went out of her head at the cemetery . . . ran all the way from the cemetery to the general superintendent's mansion. The way I heard it, Yulyona shoved past the maid and busted into the room where Charles Bonner was. She screamed at him that he was a murderer and a child killer, and then she collapsed right in front of him."

Karl stared wide-eyed at Andy, engrossed by the grim account, trying to picture his refined teacher acting like a wild woman. "So what did Charles Bonner do? Did he throw her out?"

"Throw her out! Hell, no. He put her in his automobile and drove her home—not the chauffeur, mind you, but Bonner drove the car himself. Then he carried her into her father's house, because she was groaning and sobbing and almost crazy with grief. At least that's the story I heard, and it's probably true because Veronica told me. . . .". Andy's voice trailed; he was looking around the hall. As the brother of the bride, he had responsibilities to see that the wedding celebration ran smoothly. "Hey, look, Karl, the musicians are getting ready to play. I better start moving some of the chairs back against the wall. Come on and help me."

While Karl helped move chairs, he kept glancing toward Miss Petrov until he accidentally shoved a chair leg against

Andy's ankle. Andy yelled, and Karl shifted his attention to what he was doing.

At one end of the hall, three violinists plucked their strings, tuning them. A man in a full-sleeved Slovakian shirt rested an instrument that looked like a mandolin against his hip, while an olive-skinned bass fiddler flashed smiles at all the ladies.

"They'll play the bride's dance now," Andy told Karl. "Here's your dollar bill. First Veronica will dance with Emil, then with the male family members, so you'll have to wait till all the uncles and cousins and godfathers on both sides get their turns before you can dance with her."

"How will I know when to go?" Karl asked.

"Oh, I'll come by and give you a shove. I have to leave you now, because I dance with Veronica right after Emil and my old man do."

The musicians began to play a czardas. Karl slipped into the shadows against the wall to watch Veronica and Emil Hrenko make one complete turn around the cleared floor before Mr. Stulak replaced Emil as Veronica's partner. Andy was next, then came a succession of male relatives Karl didn't know. He watched each man hand money to the best man, Emil's brother, Vaclav, before claiming a dance with the bride.

As the music went on and on, Karl tried to familiarize himself with the tempo of the czardas so that he wouldn't look clumsy when it was his turn to dance, but every few measures the musicians threw in an extra beat or took one out, confusing him. Even though each man dancing with Veronica was now limiting himself to less than half a minute, the bride's dance had gone on for nearly a quarter hour, and Veronica looked tired.

"Here you are. I couldn't find you," Andy said, coming up

to Karl in the darkened corner. "You better get out there and dance before it's over."

Karl stepped onto the floor, remembering to give the dollar to Vaclav before he cut in on a short, husky young man who was vigorously pumping Veronica's arm. "Oh, Karl," Veronica murmured when he'd put his arm around her waist, "thank you for rescuing me from Stefan."

"You look pretty," Karl told her, and she did. Exertion had brought color to her face, and the angles of her thin body seemed softened.

"I'm glad you're Andy's friend. He needs you," Veronica had time to say before a middle-aged man, hefty and bullet-headed, took Karl's place.

Although Veronica was wearing a dress of American styling, some of the little girls at the party were dressed in Slovakian costumes, with full, flowered skirts, embroidered bodices, and ribbons everywhere. They clustered around the priest when he made his way to the door, shortly after the bride's dance ended. Smiling, his hand raised as if in blessing, the priest said, "*S Bohom, S Bohom,*" to everyone. "*S Bohom,*" they replied, the men making two or three brief, shallow bows toward the departing priest. At the doorway, an elderly woman kissed the priest's hand.

After the priest had gone, the band struck up a bouncy polka, and everyone rushed to the dance floor. The polka rhythm seemed more complex to Karl than the oompa oompa he was used to in German polkas. In midstream it switched to the tempo of a czardas, then back to a polka, but speeded to such a rapid beat that the dancers panted trying to keep up. Two plump old women, dancing with each other, whirled past Karl with fast, dainty steps.

"I'm sorry I left you alone for so long," Andy said, coming at last to where Karl stood. "I had to say hello to all the guests, but now that's over, so I can stick with you. Come on, let's get a drink."

Karl expected Andy to hand him one of the bottles of soda pop cooling in tubs of ice, but instead Andy picked up a shot glass and filled it from a bottle.

"What's that?" Karl asked.

"Slivovice. Plum brandy. You can't dance at a Slovak wedding without a shot of slivovice to warm you. *Bohze daj zdrave,*" Andy said, clicking his glass against Karl's. "That's what you say when you drink with a Slovak."

"*Bohze daj zdrave,*" Karl repeated, making Andy laugh at the mangled pronunciation. Tilting his head back, Karl threw the clear liquid into his throat the way he'd seen men drink the toast at the bridal table.

Scalding fire burned a trail from Karl's throat to the middle of his chest. Shocked, he inhaled deeply through his open mouth, as though the warm air of the Sokol Hall could put out the inferno inside him.

"You better drink a beer to cool off," Andy said when he noticed Karl's watering eyes.

Trying to keep his composure, Karl gasped, "All the . . . " The words caught against his seared vocal cords. He swallowed and tried again. "All the women are dancing except Miss Petrov. Why doesn't anyone ask her to dance?"

Slowly sipping his slivovice, Andy answered, "The men feel shy around her. They're all laborers in the mill, and she's an educated woman, a teacher. In the old country, she'd be in a higher social class than they are, so they're scared to ask her for a dance."

The blazing heat in Karl's stomach subsided, radiating pleasant warmth. He relaxed.

"Why don't you ask her to dance?" Andy suggested.

"You know, I was just thinking maybe I might."

The hall had grown noisier moment by moment, and the louder it became, the more the people seemed to enjoy themselves. Karl and Andy weren't the only men who'd helped themselves to slivovice; others had been at it with more frequency and greater determination.

As Karl circled the dance floor to arrive at the place where Miss Petrov was sitting, he passed half a dozen heavy-bosomed, wide-hipped, middle-aged women standing close together and chattering at a great rate. The bridegroom's brother, Vaclav Hrenko, was halfway across the room from the women. Vaclav began a lumbering approach toward them, but they were too caught up in their conversation to notice him. Ten feet before he reached them, Vaclav stopped, lowered his head, and scuffed his feet against the floor in the manner of a bull getting ready to charge. Arms outstretched, bellowing, he hurled himself against the women like a bowling ball hitting tenpins. "I dance witta whole damn bunch a younz, alla same time," he roared.

The women screamed with laughter, some of them holding hands in front of their mouths to hide neglected teeth. "Ach! Yi, yi!" they yelled. Vaclav managed to drag three of the shrieking, convulsed women to the dance floor, where he leaped around them, slapping his heels and pretending he was going to smack their round backsides.

Karl reached Miss Petrov, expecting her to be embarrassed by Vaclav's lustiness, but she was laughing with everyone else.

"Would you care to dance, Miss Petrov?" he shouted above the laughter.

"I'd love to, Karl." She rose swiftly into his arms.

The orchestra, which seemed never to tire, began another czardas—Karl was glad he'd practiced by himself in the corner. As he'd known she'd be, Miss Petrov was a wonderful dancer. They spun around the crowded floor, bumping people and being bumped in return.

When the czardas ended Miss Petrov made no move to return to her chair, and Karl, feeling bold, put his arm around her for the next dance without even asking. A man and a woman sang harmony to the music; on the choruses, everyone joined in so wholeheartedly that the light bulbs seemed to bounce on the electric wires overhead.

Karl was exhilarated. The room throbbed with celebration; beautiful Yulyona was in his arms and seemed content to be there; his feet leaped through the dance steps as though he'd been born to them. But at the end of that dance, three husky steelworkers rushed toward them to ask Yulyona for the next. Karl had broken the ice by inviting her to the dance floor; now every man in the hall wanted to dance with her, and there were twice as many men as women.

Defeated, Karl crept back to his dark corner, but Andy intercepted him with another glass of slivovice.

"Here. You can't dance on one leg, someone told me once," Andy said, holding out the shot glass.

Karl took it and sipped slowly this time, so that the brandy's heat didn't outrage his insides, but warmed him and gave him courage. After a moment he said, "Well, I'll just have to get in line, I guess, if I want to dance with her," but Andy had already left to dance with one of his aunts.

In the next hour Karl was able to dance with Yulyona three more times, although not consecutively. Between the second and third times he'd fortified himself with another sip of slivovice, from a glass he'd poured for himself, but only half full, or maybe three-quarters. He felt wonderful—not tipsy, he assured himself, just happy.

Yulyona hadn't gone back to her chair since the time Karl first invited her to the dance floor. Man after man begged her to dance, but Karl was the swiftest, darting forward to claim her the second he sensed the music was going to stop.

Glowing color filled her cheeks; her eyes were brilliant; her off-center smile never disappeared. On his fifth or sixth dance with her—the party had lasted for hours, and Karl lost count—Vaclav Hrenko dashed out in another of his bull-like charges toward a group of women. As he passed, Vaclav bumped into Yulyona and knocked her off-balance. She stumbled against Karl, clutching his neck for support while she tried to regain her footing. As Karl held her up, he pressed her against him for a fraction of time longer than necessary. His heart beat so wildly it might have choked him if his head hadn't been floating freely in a cloud of slivovice.

"Oh, Karl, I'm sorry, forgive me for bumping into you," she said, righting herself as quickly as she could. "I have to sit down now—I'm exhausted. Would you please take me back to my chair? I'm going to catch my breath for a moment, and then I'll say good-bye to Veronica. It must be terribly late!"

The moment Karl returned her to her chair, Yulyona was surrounded by a circle of men. "No," he heard her say, "thank you, no. I can't dance any more tonight. Thank you, I just can't."

Karl knew he'd never get near her again, so he decided to go home. He could still feel the pressure of her body against his, and he wanted to savor the sensation to the fullest. Stumbling a little, Karl searched for Andy, and found him hunched forward on a bench, elbows on knees, head on hands, his fingers dug into the thick blond hair over his temples.

"Oooh, I don't feel so good," Andy moaned. "I think I drank too much."

"Will you be all right?" Karl asked. As he spoke, he noticed himself listing to the left. He concentrated to straighten his body.

"He be all right." One of Andy's aunts had brought him a cup of coffee. Gently raising his head, she eased the cup against Andy's colorless lips. "Is wedding, no?" the aunt asked Karl. "Everybody have good time. Andrej have maybe too much good time, but he be all right."

"I'm going home," Karl said, raising his voice to be heard above the buzzing in his head.

"G'night, Karl," Andy mumbled against the rim of the cup.

"G'night, Andy. It was a swell wedding. Sure was."

Outside, a few stars managed to be visible in the smoke-filled sky. Karl tried breathing deeply to clear his head, but the smoky air made him cough. He didn't care; he was delightfully happy, and pleased with his feet for taking him home the right way. "Yulyona," he sang to the stars. "Yulyona," he sighed.

"I know what I'll do!" he shouted to a rustling tree. "On Monday I'll sing my ... sonnet for her. She'll love it. I love her. Yes I do," he told the tree, whose falling leaves whispered in response.

Karl was sensible enough to take off his shoes before he climbed the stairs to his room so that he wouldn't awaken his parents. His fingers fumbled for a long time with buttons before he shed his outer clothes and crawled into bed in his underwear. Little Henry, who shared the bed, slept like a stone, which was lucky, because for what was left of the night Karl thrashed in his sleep.

His dreams blazed with Yulyona.

3

At a little past nine on the morning after the wedding, Karl walked up the hill toward the Russian Orthodox Church. Sometime during the reception the night before he'd asked someone—he couldn't remember just who it was—what time services were held at the church, and they'd told him nine o'clock.

His head felt clearer than it had at 6:00 A.M., when his mother rolled him out of bed to go to Sunday Mass at his own church. He hadn't heard any of the sermon because his thoughts were full of Yulyona, throughout Mass, during the walk home, while he ate breakfast with his family, and when he said he was going for a walk to get some fresh air.

No amount of fresh air would cure him; he was dizzy with love. For Yulyona. The many reasons why his love might be hopeless—and the main one was the difference in their ages—he refused to consider. Nothing mattered except that he was in love, for the first time in his life. He felt kinship with Andy, with Jame, with Emil Hrenko, with every other man who had ever loved a woman. Only weeks before, their behavior had seemed strange to Karl, even foolish, but now he understood.

The Russian Orthodox Church stood on the crest of a hill overlooking the bridge Karl and Jame had crossed to the Firth Sterling plant. The church's walls were wooden, its roof steeply sloped, its bell tower topped by an onion-shaped dome that supported a cross with three bars, the bottom one slanted downward. No one was outside, but Karl hid himself in a cluster of trees so that if anyone should come out, they wouldn't wonder why he was hanging around.

From where he stood he had a clear view of the Monongahela River far beneath him, and of the mills on both sides of the river. Billowing columns of steam rose from the mills' smokestacks to the dingy sky. Railroad tracks, lines and lines of them, edged the mills, and railroad cars, looking as small as match-boxes from where Karl stood, rolled along the tracks. Even at that distance, and through the deeper rumble of the laboring mills, Karl could hear the screech of the trains as they moved their loads of coal and iron ore. Next to the railroad tracks lay huge mounds of black coal that would be baked into coke, and orange ore that would become steel, mounds shaped the same as the hills that rose behind the steelworks. The trees covering the hills were grimed to the color of slate.

Karl was startled by a sudden burst of music from the Russian Orthodox Church, which must have been filled with people. A torrent of rich voices rose in words Karl couldn't understand, building minor chords to such volume that he stood motionless to give full attention to the sound. As the church bell rang, the deepest bass voice he'd ever heard—that had to be Yulyona's father, the cantor—sang alone, and then the whole congregation responded in four-part harmony. The words swelled over and over so that Karl was able to repeat them: *Hospodie pomiloi. Hospodie pomiloi.* The music impressed him so much that while it lasted he forgot he was waiting for Yulyona.

When the service ended, people streamed out of the church. Yulyona was one of the last to leave, coming out alone to walk down the hill. Karl stepped from the trees to follow her from a safe distance. He felt no guilt about stalking her secretly; he only wanted to learn where she lived so that he could walk along her street at night and perhaps catch a glimpse of her from time to time. He smiled, remembering how silly he'd thought Andy was to walk past Virginia Ward's house night after night. That was before Karl learned about love.

Yulyona was wearing a toque hat of royal-blue velvet trimmed with black feathers. The jacket of her pale-blue suit reached to her hips, and the long skirt swayed enough as she walked that he could get a good look at her ankles, which were perfect, as he already knew. Karl wondered how she could afford such nice clothes on her teacher's salary.

With a start, he noticed Yulyona turn onto Chestnut Street—Karl's street! Maybe she was going to visit the Stulaks, where the house was still filled with guests who were staying for a few extra days after the wedding. No! She passed the Stulak house and opened the gate to the Kerners' front yard. She was going into Karl's house!

He raced around the block to Pine Alley, ran through his backyard, and eased himself silently through the kitchen door. Standing still to catch his breath, he listened to the voices in the parlor: his mother's, his father's, and Yulyona's, making small talk.

"Here's our Karl now, back from his walk," Maggie Rose said when he'd gathered enough courage to enter the parlor. "Look, Karl, your teacher has come to pay us a call."

"How do, Miss Petrov," he said. His heart banged inside him as he wondered what could have possibly brought her to his house. Had she seen him following her, and come to complain to his mother and his father?

"I'm so glad you've returned, Karl," she said. "I want to talk to your parents about you, and I hoped you'd be here."

"Ab . . . about me?" Sweat broke out on his upper lip; he lowered himself into a straight chair opposite the couch where she sat.

"Yes, because next month is your birthday. November twentieth, isn't it? That's only six weeks away. I was wondering if you've reached a decision about staying in school."

"Yes," he said.

"What is your decision?"

"No."

Miss Petrov looked distressed, but Karl was so relieved that she'd come only about his staying in school that her distress didn't bother him at first. "Mr. Kerner," she said, facing Hugo, "do you approve of your son leaving school?"

"Why shouldn't I, miss?" he asked. "The mills are starting to hire again. Karl should get a job easy enough next month."

"But he's so young!"

"I was a whole lot younger than Karl when I got my first mill job," Hugo told her.

"If he would stay in school, he might become educated for some other line of work." Yulyona was trying to remain composed, but Karl could hear her voice rising.

"Why should he want other work?" Hugo asked. "Work in the steel mills ought to be pretty steady now, and the pay's decent."

"Karl has other talents," Yulyona stated. "He could become a musician."

"A musician!" Hugo's smile was condescending. "Miss

Petrov, do you know how much a musician earns? Why, we had this fellow—name of Professor Kitzweiller—come give our Kathleen piano lessons. We paid him a quarter for an hour session, and I swear, if women like my wife hadn't fed the poor man every time he came to give a lesson, he'd have starved to death. Our Kathleen says the man's a fine musician, but do you know what he's doing now? He plays piano in the nickelodeon every day. Our Kathleen only had two years of lessons, and she plays piano in the same nickelodeon each evening, for the same rate of pay Kitzweiller gets. Isn't that right, Maggie Rose?"

"Yes, Hugo, that's exactly right." Maggie Rose nodded. "Kathleen could tell you herself, Miss Petrov, only she isn't here right now. She took our little Henry to the candy store."

"Anyway," Hugo said, "Karl doesn't want to be a musician. Do you, Karl?"

"No, Pop." Music was important to Karl, but not something he'd want to work at to make a living. He used it for fun, to entertain himself and his family. "I just want to be a steelworker," he said.

"There are other professions Karl could learn," Yulyona said to Karl's parents, but with less hope.

"Like what? Pardon me for saying it in front of you, Karl, but . . ." Hugo smiled toward Miss Petrov, "the boy's no great scholar, is he? If he was a bright scholar, there'd maybe be a reason for him to stay in school, but the way he hates to study, he'd be better off going to work in the mills."

"Mill jobs are terribly dangerous," Yulyona declared.

"That's true," Maggie Rose agreed. "All the years my husband worked in the mill, before he became chief of police just three weeks ago, each day I prayed to God that he'd come home in one piece."

"Ah, Maggie Rose," Hugo said, "the danger can't be helped. It takes heat and powerful machines to make steel. But it was a good living, wasn't it? We own the house, and we always had enough to eat. On what I earned in the mill, Miss Petrov, I bought Maggie Rose a sewing machine and a washing machine. I had the house wired for electric lights, and . . . I haven't told you this before, Maggie Rose, but I'll tell you now . . . I've decided to build a bathroom indoors."

"Oh, Hugo!" Maggie Rose clasped her hands, her face lighting with gladness.

"You see, Miss Petrov," Hugo confided, as unruffled as though he were talking about the weather, "my wife's been after me for the past couple years to put a toilet in the house— gets mighty drafty out there in the outhouse on cold winter days, and the seat's cold enough to freeze a person's . . . um, excuse me, miss . . . the seat feels like a block of ice."

Karl slid downward in his chair, prickling with embarrassment.

"I always figured it was unsanitary to answer nature's call in the house," Hugo went on, "but my wife's been giving me lots of good, sound reasons why we should have a bathroom. Maggie Rose says that a flush toilet is a lot more sanitary than a full chamber pot in the bedroom at night, and I've come to believe she's right."

Karl wanted to clap his hand over his father's mouth, but if he jumped out of his chair, the people in the room would be reminded of his existence, and he preferred to remain motionless, praying for oblivion. How could his father talk about . . . *body functions!* . . . in front of Miss Petrov? How could his mother sit there smiling, looking pleased because she'd won the battle of the outhouse?

Without the faintest sign of a blush, Yulyona agreed with Hugo and Maggie Rose that yes, indeed, indoor plumbing was most desirable in a modern home. And please, she asked them, turning the conversation, would they consider the advantages of Karl remaining in school?

"As far as I'm concerned," Maggie Rose told her, "it's altogether up to Karl. We'd never rush him into the mill just to get an extra pay envelope, like some families do. In fact, we've been struggling to make him stay in school this long. And about his music," she added, "our Karl will always have that, whether he gets educated or not. You should hear him play piano, Miss Petrov. He's really good, and he never had lessons, just watched Kathleen play."

"I'd like to hear you play sometime, Karl," Yulyona told him.

"Not right now," he said in a strangled voice.

"That reminds me," she remarked, "tomorrow is the last day of the report-card period, and you've never given me your sonnet. If you have it completed, I'll take it home with me and grade it tonight."

The sonnet. He'd planned to sing it to Yulyona the following day, but now he didn't know how he'd ever face her again, let alone sing to her, after his father's earthy comments about full chamber pots and cold backsides. What must she think of the Kerners!

"I haven't finished the sonnet yet," Karl lied. "I'll turn it in for the next report-card period."

Although Karl was rigid with embarrassment, he forced

himself to stand while Miss Petrov made her good-byes. The minute the door closed behind her, he leaped up the stairs and threw himself across his bed.

The day that had begun with such happiness lay wrecked in humiliation.

4

Every day after school the following week, Kathleen taught Karl songs for the nickelodeon. Not until midweek did he learn why she was insisting on the daily lessons.

"You know, Saturday's my birthday," she mentioned while she was showing him the chords for "Hearts and Flowers" on the parlor piano.

"I almost forgot," he admitted.

"I'll be seventeen, Karl. That's a pretty important birthday. Jame wants to take me out to dinner in Pittsburgh. I told him it's up to you."

"Why up to me?"

"I can only go if you'll take my place at the nickelodeon Saturday evening." Her eyes were on the keyboard; she rubbed a speck of soot from one of the ivories. "Will you do it? You'll make fifty cents for three hours' work."

Karl considered. "Wouldn't Mom wonder where I was all that time?" he asked.

"We'll tell her the projectionist said you can come and watch him run the machine." Kathleen answered so quickly that Karl could tell she'd planned every detail. "Please, Karl, I'd really like to go to dinner with Jame. He's been doing odd jobs for Harry Ward just to earn enough money to treat me on my birthday. We'll be back on time—we'll get off the streetcar at Center Street and meet you below the middle dip the way we always do."

"What if the streetcar's late?" he asked.

"It won't be."

She raised her eyes to his. They looked so anxious that Karl said, "Sure, I'll do it for a birthday present for you, since I don't have any money to buy you anything." He'd surprise her, though. He'd use the fifty cents to buy her a gift, a day late.

"Thank you, Karl! You're the world's greatest brother." Kathleen hugged him hard, seeming so relieved that Karl was puzzled. "Now," she said, getting back to business, "let me teach you 'Love Sends a Little Gift of Roses' for the romantic scenes."

On Thursday and Friday they practiced from the time they reached home after school until Kathleen left for work, and Karl continued to practice alone in the evenings. When his mother asked him, "Why the sudden interest in piano playing?" Karl mumbled that he just felt like learning some new songs.

Saturday morning they went over the music for another hour, until Kathleen told Karl, "You're good enough. Hardly anyone pays attention to the music anyhow. The main thing you have to remember is to play loud enough to cover up the noise from the projector."

They were able to leave the house early because Maggie Rose had gone to pay the butcher's and grocer's bill, and had taken Henry with her. When they reached the nickelodeon at 5:00 P.M., Jame was already there, more dressed up than Karl had ever seen him. He wore a pin-striped suit, a striped shirt with a white collar, a narrow necktie, and a derby hat set almost straight—a surprisingly prim angle for Jame.

"Hey! You're a swell pal to do this for me and Kathleen,"

Jame said, giving Karl such a slap on the back that his teeth rattled. "I owe you a favor, buddy. Anything, anytime."

Jame was holding a package wrapped in brown paper, tied with string. "What have you got in that package?" Karl asked.

"What? This?" Jame didn't answer immediately. Then he winked at Karl and said, "What package? I don't see any package, do you?" so Karl supposed it was a birthday present for Kathleen.

"We better get down to the streetcar stop," Jame said, taking Kathleen's arm. "Bye, Karl. Thanks a lot, kid."

Kathleen hesitated, and turned back toward Karl as though she wanted to tell him something. He waited, but all she said was, "Good-bye, Karl." The two of them hurried away.

They looked so nice together. Karl wished he could be all dressed up like that, going out on a date with Yulyona, holding her arm possessively. Since he had the better part of an hour to kill before reporting to the nickelodeon, he strolled along First Street, hands in his pockets. The sky was so dark with mill smoke that the lighted interiors of the stores seemed inviting; he peered through the windows, hoping that by some stroke of luck Yulyona might be inside one of the stores.

All that week at school, Karl had studied Yulyona closely to discover any change in her attitude toward him, fearing that his father's outhouse comments might have lowered her regard for all the Kerners. She seemed to think no less of him, though, and Karl felt relieved.

Slowly the relief turned to hurt. Karl had expected Yulyona to treat him in a special way, after that night they'd danced together. Surely the feeling hadn't all been on his side—she *must* have felt something for him, to dance with him the way she had. In class he paid meticulous attention to the words she spoke, the gestures she used, anxiously searching for some sign that she favored him. But there was none. Yulyona was unfailingly warm toward Karl, considerate of his feelings, interested in his opinions of the literature they read; what bothered him was that she was just as interested, considerate, and warm toward bubble-headed Virginia Ward, slow-witted Tilly Horner, smug Fred Hollingsted, and every other student in the sophomore homeroom.

Karl became frantic to gain her attention. Each night when he was supposedly meeting Kathleen at the nickelodeon, he would go to the library to take a shower so he'd look immaculate for Yulyona. Each morning he spent so many minutes combing his hair in front of his mother's mirror that Kathleen teased him about having a girlfriend, although she had no idea that Karl was in love with Yulyona. He hadn't told anyone.

That week he studied literature and grammar harder than he'd ever studied anything in his life, so that he could sound intelligent in class. It didn't help. Nothing helped. Yulyona treated him no differently than she had before the wedding reception.

Love was certainly more complex than he'd anticipated on that day he saw Jame and Kathleen kissing in the gazebo, and had thought it might be nice to fall in love. The physical feeling was as exciting as he'd imagined—that twist in the viscera, heat in the blood—but there was more to it than just physical feeling. There was his eagerness to see her, which made him run most of the way to school each morning; his longing to have her meet his eyes in class, so he could search her eyes for a sign that she loved him; his thrill when she read love poems aloud in her stirring voice, and he listened intently so that he could bend the meaning of each line to fit the two of them.

And there was his anguish ... the time she got into a long discussion, which she obviously enjoyed, with Fred Hollingsted about the inner meaning of some lines of verse, and Karl couldn't understand what they were talking about.

Each day he loved her more. But he didn't know how to make her love him back. He decided that the difference in their ages caused her to think of him as a mere boy, not as a man.

Karl began to imagine ways he could make himself appear adult to Yulyona. Outside the post office, a recruiting poster showed a tall, muscular soldier in a U.S. Army uniform, holding a bayonet-tipped rifle. If Karl were to lie about his age, he could probably join the army. He pictured himself in uniform, waiting outside the high school for Yulyona to come out. When she saw him, she would realize that he was a man, and then she'd begin to respond to his love for her. The trouble with this fantasy was that if Karl joined the army, he'd have to leave Canaan and Yulyona. Anyway, he didn't want to be a soldier. He wanted to be a steelworker.

5

At ten to six by the clock on the Canaan City Bank, Karl approached the ticket booth outside the nickelodeon. "I'm Karl Kerner," he told the manager, who was talking to the ticket seller. "I'm Kathleen's brother."

"Oh yeah," the manager muttered around the stub of a cigar. "She told me you was gonna play tonight. We got three films on the program—*At Jones' Ferry, The New York Hat,* and a western. Here's a cue sheet that come with *At Jones' Ferry*. We didn't get no cue sheets for the other two."

Kathleen hadn't mentioned anything about cue sheets–Karl didn't know what they were. He took the piece of paper the manager handed him and studied it uncertainly.

"Musical Plot for *At Jones' Ferry,*" it read:

1. Country dance till stop dancing.
2. Lively till Boss Strikes Young Jones.
3. Moderato till girl falls in river.
4. Agitato–long, till subtitle "A Chance for Revenge."
5. Crescendo till girl is rescued, then:
6. Waltz or lively till finish.

Karl's apprehension grew as he read the list. *Moderato, agitato, crescendo*–were they the names of songs? If so, he didn't know a single one of them. He'd have to fake it. Kathleen had said the manager had a tin ear; Karl fervently hoped that was true.

The Intermission slide was showing on the screen when he entered the dark theater. As he pushed his way along a row of seats, he passed through the beam from the projector, making his own silhouette follow him across the letters of *Intermission.* He reached the piano to the right of the screen just as Professor Kitzweiller was putting on his hat. The man sagged with weariness.

"Ah, Karl," Professor Kitzweiller said, "Kathleen told me you were going to play for her tonight. Ach, and you never even took piano lessons. How fitting, considering this vulgar entertainment. In Berlin I conducted *Tannhauser.* Now I sit ten hours each day to play idiocy for dancing shadows." He spat in disgust, just as the slide on the screen changed to "Please Don't Spit on the Floor."

"So long, Professor," Karl called softly as the man faded into the darkness.

Karl sat down, then stood up to spin the piano seat to a lower height. Seated again, he flexed his fingers, feeling nervous and scared. The piano keys showed only dimly in the pale light. Feet shuffled as people entered and left the theater; the sign on the screen changed to Those Not Having Seen the Entire Program Can Remain for the Next Show. Behind him, Karl heard coughing and a lot of conversation in foreign languages.

With a clattery whir, the projector started to roll, and the title *The New York Hat* appeared on the screen. Karl struck a chord, waiting for the first scene—there it was: A woman lying in bed, apparently dying. What could he play for a deathbed scene? He hit the same chord again, then, in desperation, began to play "I'll Take You Home Again, Kathleen" because he couldn't think of anything better. Expecting snickers from the audience, he waited tensely, but the audience remained silent. When he stole a quick glance at the theatergoers—he could see only the people in the first two rows—they were staring at the screen, their expressions rapt.

Karl relaxed a little. The theater seemed filled with immigrants mostly, people like Andy Stulak's parents, who had no need to understand English to appreciate the drama of silent films. Since they were unfamiliar with the American tunes Karl was playing, they wouldn't know whether the songs fit the scenes or not.

A sigh of approval rose from the audience as Mary Pickford appeared on the screen. Karl had seen her in a movie several months earlier, and remembered her because of her long blond curls. Playing opposite Mary Pickford was a handsome young actor named Lionel Barrymore. During their third scene Karl got to use "Hearts and Flowers."

When *At Jones' Ferry* came on, he disregarded the cue sheet and played "Alexander's Ragtime Band" for the barn dance. No one in the theater seemed to mind. After that he played whatever popular tunes came into his head, banging the keys loudly as Kathleen had instructed him to do, because the projector really was noisy.

All three of the one-reel films were shown in little more than half an hour, and then were repeated again and again as fresh patrons arrived to replace the ones who'd left the theater. By nine o'clock, Karl's eyes hurt, his head ached, his fingers tingled like pins and needles, and his neck had a crick in it from turning to watch the screen. How could Kathleen keep it up night after night, Karl wondered. Even worse, how could poor Professor Kitzweiller last for ten straight hours every day? Karl felt a wave of relief when the projector stopped and the lights went on. Blinking patrons buttoned their coats and headed for the door—Karl was right behind them.

He was more exhausted after three hours of piano playing than he'd been after a whole day in the rolling mill. It was a tense kind of exhaustion, not the satisfying kind that came from moving three tons of steel. If he'd ever considered becoming a musician (and he hadn't, except in his unrealistic dreams of ways to make Yulyona notice him), those three hours in the nickelodeon would have squelched the desire. The manager didn't even say Karl had done a good job—just handed him a half dollar on his way out of the theater.

As the chilly air revived him on the mile-long walk to

Center Street, he decided that the job had one compensation after all—when he got home he could describe the three movies to his mother. He'd seen the subtitles so often that he'd memorized most of them.

At the bottom of Center Street, Karl waited beside the streetcar tracks for Kathleen and Jame, but the streetcar didn't come. Maybe it had arrived early, he thought. Climbing Center Street, he looked for Kathleen and Jame in the shadows. They weren't there. Instead, Francis X Culley stood leaning against the lamppost on the middle dip.

"Francis X, what are you doing here?" Karl asked him.

"I got a message for you." Perhaps it was because of the harsh illumination from the street light, but Francis X looked even sneakier than usual.

"What's the message?" Karl asked. "Who's it from?"

"Here." Francis X handed him an envelope.

Examining it, Karl saw that the flap had been torn open and sloppily resealed. "Did you open this?" he demanded to know.

Francis X backed out of reach as he answered, "Huh-uhn, I never opened it. Honest Injun!"

Karl undid the envelope and pulled out a folded piece of paper. The street light was bright enough that he could see the words clearly:

> Dear Family,
> By the time you read this, Jame and I will be married. I'm sorry it had to happen this way, but you gave us no choice, Mom. Don't blame Karl. He knew nothing about it.
> Kathleen

He crumpled the paper in his fist, feeling as though the breath had been knocked out of him. Why hadn't he guessed? The signs had been so obvious! Kathleen's nervousness, her carefully laid plans, Jame's evasion about the package he was carrying—it must have held their clothes.

How was Karl going to face his parents with this news?

Grinning devilishly, Francis X inched forward. "Me and you is brother-in-laws now, huh, Karl?"

"So you *did* open it, you bugger!" With a bellow of rage, Karl chased Francis X the rest of the way up Center Street and Pine Alley, but his rage was so weighted with despair that he couldn't catch the boy before Francis X escaped through the Culleys' back gate.

Outside his own gate, Karl stood for a long time, dreading what he had to do. "Don't blame Karl," Kathleen had written in the note, but who else were his parents to blame? It was with Karl's compliance that Kathleen and Jame had met night after night for the past two months. Karl had deceived his mother just as much as Kathleen had.

His steps dragged across the back porch. Maggie Rose must have heard them, because when he opened the door, she yelled, "Surprise!" She was bent over the kitchen table, smiling broadly as she lit candles on a birthday cake. "Happy Birthday to you," Maggie Rose sang in her strident voice. "Happy Birthday . . . " She stopped when she realized Kathleen wasn't behind Karl. "Where's your sister?"

The note was still balled in his hand. Reluctantly, he gave it to his mother.

Her cry was so anguished it brought Hugo running from the parlor. Maggie Rose collapsed on the floor, hugging her knees and rocking as she wept in harsh, tortured wails.

"What's the matter?" Hugo yelled, still holding a box tied in bright green ribbon—Kathleen's birthday gift from her parents. Karl took the box from his father before handing him the note.

When Hugo read the note, he winced as though he'd been struck. After throwing the note on the table, he bent to haul Maggie Rose off the floor as he would a sack of coal, and deposited her in a kitchen chair. Then he circled the table to grab Karl by the lapels.

"All right, son," he shouted. "What's this all about?"

Trembling, Karl told how he'd taken Kathleen's job in the nickelodeon that evening. "I didn't know she was going to run off and get married. Honest, Pop! She just said Jame was taking her out to dinner." He was too frightened to admit that he'd let Jame walk Kathleen home nightly for two whole months.

"Where did she say they were going?" Hugo demanded, his jaw grim.

"To Pittsburgh. That's all she told me."

Slowly, the anger drained from Hugo's big body. His shoulders drooped. "Then there's no way we can find them," he said, releasing Karl.

Maggie Rose lay against the kitchen table like a broken doll, her head slumped on her arms. "My Kathleen," she sobbed. "My Kathleen. My baby girl—gone, gone forever."

"Maggie Rose, stop your crying," Hugo said, his voice gentle. "You're carrying on like Kathleen's dead. She isn't gone forever. She's just gotten married."

"She was only seventeen," Maggie Rose wailed, using the past tense as though Kathleen were only a memory.

"Kathleen's not the first girl in Canaan to get married at

seventeen, and she won't be the last," Hugo told her, but Maggie Rose refused to be comforted. She keened like a mourner at an Irish wake. Karl was shaken by the harsh sounds of his mother's pain, which reminded him of her terrible grieving after Kurt and Kara died.

"Go to bed," his father barked at him, and Karl ran upstairs as fast as he could, tearing off his clothes to crawl under the blankets beside Henry, who slept undisturbed. Karl covered his head with the pillow to block the sound of his mother's weeping, but he could still hear it, and it lasted for hours.

Sunlight streaming through the window awakened him. No one had roused him to go to seven o'clock Mass, and the brightness of the sun showed that it was much later than seven. Henry was gone from the bed. After Karl dressed, he crept to the top of the stairs and glanced into his parents' bedroom. Hugo was asleep, with his thick arm, encased in gray, long-sleeved underwear, across his eyes. Maggie Rose was not beside him.

Treading softly in his stocking feet, Karl descended the stairs. Maggie Rose sat in her chair next to the kitchen window, rocking back and forth, staring straight ahead. She wore the same clothes she'd worn the night before; Karl knew she hadn't been to bed. Never before had Karl known his mother to deliberately miss Sunday Mass, and this frightened him as much as her stony, haggard expression.

At her feet, Henry sat in his nightgown, whimpering, "Mom, I'm hungry. Get me something to eat, Mom." Maggie Rose ignored the child as if he didn't exist.

"Don't bother Mom," Karl said, picking up Henry to carry him across the room to the table. "Here, sit still and keep quiet. I'll get you some jelly bread."

Karl spread two slices of bread thick with grape jelly to mollify Henry. He cut bacon and laid it across the cast-iron frying pan, then built a fire in the stove. The bacon was sputtering noisily by the time his father came into the kitchen. Hugo looked at Maggie Rose, shook his head, and sat down at the table.

"Do you know how to make coffee?" he asked Karl.

"No."

"Neither do I."

Getting to her feet as stiffly as a marionette, Maggie Rose left her rocker and lifted down the blue enamel coffeepot. When the pot was filled and set on the stove, she took the fork from Karl's hand, shoved him aside, and began to turn the bacon. All the while she fried eggs and filled plates for her men, she remained silent.

"Aren't you going to eat?" Hugo asked her, but she returned to her rocker without answering.

Karl cleared the table and washed the dishes. After the kitchen was clean, he dug through his mother's sewing basket for a big button. When he found one the right size, he looped string through the holes to make a whirly-twirly for Henry, who was upset by his mother's cold withdrawal.

After breakfast Hugo had gone to buy the Pittsburgh *Post Gazette*, and returned to sit at the table paging through the newspaper while Karl read the funnies to Henry. Maggie Rose never moved from her rocker. As the hours dragged on, the house sank deeper in gloom.

A knock on the kitchen door at midafternoon made Karl jump as though he'd heard a cannon shot. He opened the door to find Bridey Culley standing on the porch, her shoulders wrapped in a shawl.

"I'm wantin' to come inside, Karl," she told him.

"Sure." He stepped back to let her enter, uncertain whether Maggie Rose would react with anger to a visit from Jame's mother, or whether she'd continue to rock, staring at the wall, and ignore Bridey Culley along with everyone else.

After a nod toward Hugo, Bridey crossed the kitchen to stand before Maggie Rose. "It's done and over now, Maggie Rose, and there's no turnin' back the clock," she said. "Jame has taken Kathleen to wife. I want you to know I had nary an inkling what they were up to. Nor did Mayo. Only our Francis Xavier knew, the little scamp, and he kept his gab shut for once."

Maggie Rose raised her head as though the movement pained her. "Where are they?" she whispered.

"They come over to our house just a bit ago. That moment's when we first learned they was wed. All last night we could hear you carryin' on, Maggie Rose, clear to our house, but we didn't know what ailed you, and we'd liefer not come find out on account of how you feel about us. When I told Kathleen, just now, how you'd wailed the night through, she wept her pretty eyes out, poor little love. So I said I'd come to this house and try to make peace atwixt yez two. And it'd be a poor thing if we didn't make peace atwixt our two families as well, now that our childer are wed. This hate has gone on long enough."

Maggie Rose stared at Bridey with haunted eyes for a long moment. Then, with startling suddenness, she shrieked, "I want my daughter back!"

Hugo jumped from his chair, then sat down again. Karl hushed Henry, who'd been frightened by his mother's harsh cry.

"I want my girl!" Maggie Rose cried again.

"You can't have her back to keep, because she's Jame's wife now," Bridey said, as though she were speaking to a child. "But you can give her a mother's blessing, that she needs so desperate." Hesitantly, she placed her hand on Maggie Rose's shoulder. "Our Jame is a decent lad, and he loves your girl so much, my dear. Don't shut them out of your heart."

With a moan, Maggie Rose threw herself against Bridey's soft body and began to sob. Bridey's arms went swiftly around the weeping woman.

"I was wrong," Maggie Rose lamented. "God forgive me, I was wrong and mean and hateful. God has punished my hard heart by taking my daughter away."

"Whisht, now, God hasn't punished you, love," Bridey soothed her, "and he hasn't taken away your girl. I'm guessin' she's outside your door this minute, her and her husband. Will you let them in?"

"Yes!" The assent tore from Maggie Rose's chest in a sob.

Wiping her eyes with her shawl, Bridey said, "Karl, lad, throw open your door to see who might be on the stoop."

Karl did, and Kathleen flew across the room to her mother. Jame slipped through the door and pressed himself against the wall as though he hoped to make his large frame less conspicuous, but Hugo went up to him and threw an arm around Jame's shoulders.

"What's happening?" Henry cried. "I don't know what's going on, do you?"

"Be quiet a little while longer," Karl whispered. "I'll explain everything later."

Kathleen and Maggie Rose clung to each other. It seemed to Karl, because his mother was so much shorter, that Kathleen was the parent comforting a sorrowful child.

After a moment, Bridey approached Jame and said softly, "It's a grand lass she is, Jame, and I'm thinkin' it'll all work out fine, God be thanked. I'll go home now, so you can talk with your new in-laws for a bit."

"You're a grand lass too, Ma," he said, touching the curve of her cheek with his finger. "You're a real peach."

"Peach, is it! Save your blarney for your bride," she bantered, but she flushed with pleasure.

Hugo told her, "What Jame said is true, Bridey. It was good of you to come. You're a fine woman."

"Providence and mercy! I'd best get out of here before me head's turned. Good day to this house." Bridey skittered through the door and pulled it shut behind her.

Kathleen's arms were still around Maggie Rose as she whispered something in her mother's ear. Maggie Rose hesitated, then straightened her back and marched across the kitchen floor, her hand outstretched toward Jame. Standing before him, her head thrown back so she could look up at his great height, she moved her lips as though she were searching for words to say to him, but couldn't think of the right ones.

Instead of taking her hand, Jame swept Maggie Rose high in his arms and whirled her around the room.

"For the love of God, put me down, you great lummox," she cried, but before Jame did, she kissed his grinning face. "You're a giant of a man," she gasped, staggering a little when he set her on her feet. "You're as strong as Hugo when he was your age."

"Well!" Hugo said, rubbing his hands. "I think we should all sit down and talk things over. Maggie Rose, Kathleen, Jame, sit around the kitchen table. Karl, you and Henry stay too."

"*Now* can I know what's happening?" Henry begged.

Kathleen leaned from her chair to hug her little brother. "Jame and I are married," she told him.

"Oh, is that all," Henry said.

"What I want to know," Maggie Rose declared, "is who married you two."

"A justice of the peace in Pittsburgh," Kathleen answered.

"Then you've got to be married by a priest right away."

"We will, Mom. We'll go to see Father Kilkenny tomorrow, as soon as Jame gets home from work."

"From work? You've found a job then, Jame?" Hugo asked.

"I wouldn't have married Kathleen if I hadn't," he told them. "I start tomorrow in the twenty-eight-inch billet mill at the Canaan Works. And I want you to know, Mom and Pop Kerner . . ." Jame smiled, calling them that for the first time, " . . . that I'll play it straight from now on, both on the job and off. No more cuttin' up, honest to God. I'm a married man now, and I'm gonna make Kathleen proud of me."

Hugo cleared his throat. "What about your parents? Won't they need the money you earn?"

"My dad's doing some work for Harry Ward," Jame answered, "at least till the election's over. In fact, my old man's turning into a regular Irish politician."

"Uh . . . can I ask one thing?" Karl touched Kathleen's hand to get her attention, because she was gazing at Jame with a rapt, adoring expression. "What about tomorrow night at the nickelodeon?"

"What about it?"

"Am I supposed to play again?"

"No, silly, I'll be playing as usual," she told him. "I'm not going to give up my job—Jame and I need to save money for furniture. We've rented a furnished room for now, on Grant

Avenue right near the nickelodeon, but we want to get an apartment as soon as we can. So I'll work till I get pregnant, and I hope that won't be too soon."

"Kathleen!" Hugo looked shocked. He could talk about outhouses without a qualm of self-consciousness, but to hear a young woman mention pregnancy! That was indecent!

"Sorry, Pop. Anyway, I'm going to keep working." She became a bit wistful. "It will seem strange, not going to school tomorrow. But—since married women aren't even allowed to teach in Canaan High School, they sure as shootin' aren't going to let a married girl stay in school."

"I'm not certain that I approve of your working," Maggie Rose said. "Now that you're a married woman . . . " She saddened for an instant, using that term to describe her daughter, but quickly raised her chin and went on, "You should stay home to take care of your husband and housework."

"Mom, you're as old-fashioned as the Canaan School Board. That's why they won't let women teach when they're married, because they're supposed to keep house and let their husbands support them. How archaic!" Kathleen declared. "This is 1912, Mom. The whole world's changing."

Karl watched his mother struggle to choke back her objections. Maggie Rose's whole world, at least, had changed drastically, and in less than a day. She was doing her best to accept Kathleen's marriage, and to shed her hostility toward the Culleys. Karl was proud of her.

"Congratulations, Mom," he said, patting her hand.

Maggie Rose looked surprised. "What for?"

"Oh . . . you know," he invented quickly. "People always congratulate the mother of the bride, don't they?"

"Thank you," she said, sounding a bit dubious, as though

losing her daughter wasn't something she especially wanted to be congratulated on. Then, with forced cheerfulness, Maggie Rose poked Karl's arm and joked, "Now don't you go getting married on me! Don't *you* go falling in love!" She laughed as if she thought the possibility were as unlikely as a frost in August.

Henry shouted, "Look! Karl's face is turning all red."

"Well, for Pete's sake!" Kathleen exclaimed. "I've had a hunch that Karl might be sweet on some girl."

"You and me better have a heart-to-heart talk about spoonin', Karl," Jame teased.

Hugo chuckled and asked, "Who is she, son? Is it some little girl we all know?"

Their amusement embarrassed Karl, and annoyed him even more; he could feel the hot blood stinging his cheeks. They acted as though Kathleen, by getting married, had become a woman entitled to adult love, while Karl was just a kid with a schoolboy crush. Kathleen was only a year older than he was!

"Believe me," Karl muttered in protest, "there are no little girls in my life."

That was the truth. Karl loved a woman, a splendid and beautiful woman.

CHAPTER FIVE

TEMPERED STEEL

1

Karl thought about Yulyona, if not all the time, then most of the time.

At Mass on the first Sunday of November, an idea came to him like a revelation. He recognized it as the perfect method to win Yulyona's affection.

It was during the offertory prayers, while Father Kilkenny intoned the Latin words "... *sic fiat sacrificium nostrum in conspectu hodie, Ut placeat tibi....*" Karl was following the English translation in his missal: "... grant that the sacrifice which we offer this day in your sight may be pleasing to you...."

That's when it hit him.

A sacrifice!

If Karl were to make a really big sacrifice for Yulyona, she'd have to acknowledge his feelings. And if she knew that the sacrifice was the most selfless offering Karl was capable of giving her, Yulyona might be so moved she'd begin to love him.

Although the idea stirred him with excitement, sadness had already begun to weigh on him, because he knew without thinking what the sacrifice would have to be. Karl possessed only one offering of enough magnitude to impress Yulyona: the goal he'd been heading for all his life, the ambition that was almost in his grasp. His desire to be a steelworker.

His hesitation lasted only a moment. By the time Father Kilkenny chanted the Sanctus, Karl had made the decision to remain in school. Because he loved her, he would offer Yulyona a sacrifice he knew would be pleasing to her. His entire future.

Karl had a strong impulse to get up right then, in the middle of Mass, and go tell Yulyona that he planned to stay in school. But he still didn't know where she lived. Anyway, timing would be of great importance to get the most impact from his announcement, so he shouldn't just go and blurt it out. He'd have to plan, pick the time and set the scene to achieve the best possible effect.

The perfect time would be his sixteenth birthday, two and a half weeks away. That would give him a chance to figure out a more pleasant setting than the chalk-dust-filled classroom, and to think of a way to persuade her to enter the pleasant setting when he found one.

He was so wrapped in his thoughts that he was startled to discover the Mass had ended. "Put my muffler on me," Henry whispered. The little boy was already in the aisle, handing Karl the child-sized woolen scarf Maggie Rose had knitted. Karl tied the scarf, then followed Henry out of the church.

From the top of the church steps, Karl looked down on the Canaan Works of the Carnegie Steel Company, spread for miles along the west bank of the Monongahela River. He sighed deeply, relinquishing it all. Whatever Yulyona wanted him to become, he would become. For her.

If only she would love him a little, in return for his sacrifice.

2

"Karl, go out and get some wood," his mother told him two days later, on the evening of election day. "It's turning so cold outside that I want to keep the stove going all night. Put on your coat!" she called as he opened the kitchen door.

"I don't need a coat just to go to the woodshed," he hollered back, shutting the door behind him.

The first snow of the season had begun to fall in early afternoon, and lay on the ground an inch deep, too fresh to be sullied by soot. Karl admired his footprints in the snow; they were much larger than they'd been the winter before. Maggie Rose complained that his last two pairs of shoes were hardly broken in before he outgrew them, even though he'd worn them until they squeezed his toes.

Shivering, he entered the darkness of the woodshed. As he bent to pick up a stack of kindling, a heavy touch on his shoulder made him shriek with fright and scatter the wood.

"Take it easy," Andy whispered. "It's only me."

"For cripes sake, Andy, you scared the hell out of me! What are you doing out here?"

"Keep quiet, will you? I don't want anyone to hear us."

Karl had been about to yell at Andy for frightening him out of a year's growth, but in the pale shaft of light that invaded the shed, he saw Andy's face. "What happened?" he asked, aware that something was seriously wrong.

"I've been hiding here since I got home from work," Andy

told him, sounding miserable. "I was hoping you'd come out so I could tell you I'm leaving."

"Leaving? Where? What for?"

"I would have left last night," Andy said, "only I didn't have any money, so I worked all day today and picked up my pay. There's a P and LE freight train that comes through Canaan at ten o'clock tonight. I'm gonna hop it."

"Lord, Andy, come on inside the house where it's warm and tell me what this is all about."

"No!" Andy shook Karl's hand off his sleeve. "I don't want anybody to know where I am or what I'm doing. Only you. I can't stand staying in Canaan any longer."

Andy turned so that he stood in shadow, but the outline of his body revealed his tenseness. "Last night," he said, "Harry Ward caught me kissing Virginia out by their front gate. He threw a fit, as you can imagine. Then he dragged me home to my folks, shooting off his mouth that no fresh hunky kid was gonna mess around with Harry Ward's daughter, and if my father wanted to keep his job in the mill, he'd better lock me up tight inside the house every night."

"The big sap!" Karl cried. "Did your father tell him to go fall on himself?"

"My old man? Hah! Fat chance. You know, Harry Ward sure picked the right threat to scare my father gutless. No, my old man didn't say a word. He just hauled down my pants and beat my bare dupa with a belt, right in front of Harry Ward."

"Oh, Andy!" Karl felt sick, visualizing the scene—Andy being beaten to appease Harry Ward. No words came to his mind that could console Andy for such a humiliation. If Andy were skipping town because he'd been told to stay away from

Virginia Ward, Karl could maybe talk him out of that—Virginia Ward simply wasn't worth the trouble. But to be stripped and flogged in front of that stuffed-shirt vote-grubber Harry Ward—if that had happened to Karl, he'd probably leave town too. But he didn't want to lose Andy.

"How can your folks manage without your wages?" he tried, hoping that might be a good argument to keep Andy home.

"They'll manage. My father found four new boarders on the day of Veronica's wedding. He'll probably get someone to fill my bed before the sheets are cold," Andy replied bitterly.

"What about your mother? You'll break her heart."

"That can't be helped." Andy's voice was rough. "Look, I know what you're trying to do, Karl. You're trying to change my mind. Well, it won't work, so cut it out or I'll beat it right now, without waiting for the ten o'clock freight."

"No, don't do that." Karl caught Andy's arm and held it tightly this time. "Where are you planning to head for?"

"Wherever the train goes. I'll stay here in your shed to keep out of the cold till it's time for the freight. After that . . . I don't know when we'll see each other again, so it's good-bye." Though the outside light was dim, Karl could see Andy's lips tremble.

"Not yet it's not good-bye," Karl said. "Listen, I have to get inside now before my mom wonders what happened to me, but I'll bring out some food in a little while. It's bad enough you're freezing out here; you don't want to starve too. I'll be back as soon as I can. Just stay right here, all right?"

"Don't forget to take in the wood," Andy reminded him.

"Oh yeah. Now don't go anywhere before I get back. Promise me you won't." When Andy nodded, Karl grabbed an armload of wood and ran back through the snowflakes, which were beginning to fall more thickly.

"Saints in heaven, what did you do, chop down a whole tree?" Maggie Rose asked when he stomped into the kitchen.

"I had to use the outhouse," he lied. "When will supper be ready?"

"As soon as your father gets home. For the past week, I never know when he's going to get here—he's stayed late reading those department reports each evening. At least when he was in the mill, he came home on time." She poked the potatoes with a fork, then told Karl, "Go wake Henry and wash his hands and face. He fell asleep on the couch."

While Karl lathered his brother with the washrag at the kitchen sink, he was so preoccupied wondering what he should do about Andy that he rubbed Henry's face too hard.

"Owww!" Henry squealed. "Mom, make Karl stop bending my nose. He's hurting me."

"Karl, be gentler with your little brother," Maggie Rose chided him. "I remember when you were little, you hated getting your face washed so much that you used to hide under the porch. I couldn't squeeze under the porch after you, so I used to send Kathleen, and she'd drag you out, even though she was just a little tyke herself." The steak sizzled louder as Maggie Rose speared it and turned it over in the frying pan. "Kathleen and Jame are coming for supper tomorrow night, since Jame is on day turn this week. Did I tell you that?"

"You told me," Karl muttered, hardly hearing her chatter. As he gave Henry's face a final swipe with the towel, he tried to decide what he could say to Andy to make him give up the foolish idea of running away. He'd have to come up with something convincing.

From the Stulak back porch, Andy's mother began to call "Andrej, Andrej," over and over. Her forlorn cry penetrated the Kerners' kitchen and made Karl's chest ache. Should he run out that minute and tell her where Andy was, what he was planning? Karl always found it hard to communicate with Mrs. Stulak because she understood so little English, and he didn't dare tell Andy's father. Andy would get a far worse beating, and would hate Karl for betraying him. If only Veronica were still home!

Heavy footsteps on the porch made Maggie Rose's face brighten. "Here's your father now. It's a good thing he's home— this steak is getting dried out like a shoe sole."

Hugo entered the kitchen, shaking snow from his overcoat. For the second time in an hour, Karl saw a look of despair, this one on his father's face.

"Mother of God, you look like the world died," Maggie Rose exclaimed as she hurried to take Hugo's coat. "Sit down and tell me what's bothering you."

"Put supper on the table," Hugo said. "I'll tell you while I'm eating. Come over here, Karl, and start to eat."

"What about me?" Henry asked. "I need to eat, too, Pop. I'm hungry."

"You sit at this table, eat your food, and don't say a single word," Hugo told him. "And if you don't mind me, you'll go right to bed without your supper. Hear?"

Henry nodded, taken aback by his father's uncustomary sternness.

Hugo propped his elbows on the table and rested his head on his hands. As Maggie Rose set his plate before him, he said, "It's a strange thing that's happening, Maggie Rose, and I don't know what to make of it."

"Tell me." She heaped his plate with potatoes and gravy, then slipped into her chair to wait for his explanation.

Hugo began, "Mayo Culley came to see me today."

"Is something wrong with Jame?" Maggie Rose asked quickly.

"No, it has nothing to do with Jame. Except . . . do you remember when Jame told us that Mayo is working for Harry Ward? That . . . that's what makes me think there's a fly in the ointment."

"For Lord's sake, Hugo, begin at the beginning!"

"All right." Hugo took a mouthful of steak and talked around it. "Mayo Culley came to me today, and I never saw a man look so tormented about what he had to say. He looked like he wanted to bawl."

"Big people don't bawl," Henry said. "Babies bawl." He quieted when Hugo shook a warning finger at him.

"So what did Mayo say?" Maggie Rose prompted.

"He told me there's supposed to be a big gambling party tonight at the general superintendent's mansion. Charles Bonner and his friends are going to play poker while they wait for the election returns. Mayo said he heard it from Mary Margaret, who has to work late tonight to serve the food."

"Well, what's so awful about that?" Maggie Rose asked, puzzled.

"Don't you see?" Hugo threw down his fork. "Mayo knew I'd be honor-bound, as chief of police, to have a gambling party raided, no matter whose house it's in. But my horse sense tells me it isn't Mayo who wanted me to know about the gambling. It's Harry Ward. It's him who sent Mayo to me with the information."

Maggie Rose shook her head, and Karl was equally puzzled. "Why would Harry Ward want the superintendent's mansion raided, Pop?" he asked.

"I haven't pieced it all together myself," Hugo replied slowly. "Eat your supper, Karl. I started to get suspicious when I told the police officers at city hall that they'd have to make the raid. Five minutes later, one of the men tripped and said he'd sprained his ankle, so he went home. Right after that, another officer told me he'd just got a message that his wife was took bad sick, and he left. The third officer said that since the voting polls had just closed, the lockup was sure to start filling up with drunks, so he'd better stay at the jail. The other officers were out walking their beats, and that left no one but me to stage the raid."

Hugo took a deep breath and slumped in his chair. "It was the look on their faces, Maggie Rose. Ashamed, but scared. Harry Ward's setting me up, I'm pretty sure."

"Then don't go." She leaned across the table. "I don't understand it, but don't go."

"I think Harry Ward wants to get rid of me, now that the elections are over," Hugo said. "I've made him nervous since I started poking around in the police department records, but he needed an honest man as police chief as long as the campaign was going on. Well, the voting's all over now. If I raid a gambling party at the superintendent's mansion tonight, Ward will somehow—and I'm not sure just how—use that as an excuse to get rid of me."

"Then why are you going?" Maggie Rose asked.

"Because I'm still chief of police!" Hugo cried. "It's my duty to enforce the law. Karl, I intend to deputize you to go with me."

"You'll not take our boy!" Maggie Rose shouted. "Make those cowardly policemen go with you."

"No, I won't force the men to risk their jobs. I'll not make them do what I dread to do myself. Karl won't be in any danger, Maggie Rose. I just need him as a witness to the arrests."

"Arrests! You mean you'd really arrest Charles Bonner and his friends?" Maggie Rose was incredulous. "Hugo, don't do it! They'll crucify you!"

"I know." Hugo sighed. "And poor Mayo Culley had to be the Judas. I feel sorry for the man."

"Sorry for Mayo?" Maggie Rose exploded. "What about sorry for Hugo?"

"My dear, I have two strong hands. I can find a job of work anywhere. Mayo has only one good hand. He has to do what Harry Ward tells him to, or lose the first job he's had in years."

Maggie Rose stared at him for a long time. "You're a fool, Hugo," she said. "A sainted fool. Make sure to dress warm when you go out. And Karl, wear your galoshes. It's bitter outside."

Karl suddenly remembered Andy, alone in the cold woodshed. Throwing on his coat, he said, "Pop, give me just a minute. I have to run to the outhouse."

"Are you getting sick?" his mother asked him. "You just went a little while ago."

"I'll be right back." Karl raced through the backyard and pushed open the door to the woodshed. "Andy, something came up. I have to go out with my pop for a while, but it's not even eight o'clock yet, so I ought to be back in plenty of time before you leave." He *had* to get back, because he had to stop Andy from leaving on that train.

"Just hurry," Andy said through chattering teeth.

Then, because he was nervous, Karl really did have to use the outhouse. To save time, he rebuttoned his pants while he was hurrying back to the house.

"Look at all that snow on you," Maggie Rose scolded. "Pull your cap down farther over your ears, and button your overcoat all the way up. You too, Hugo. What a night to go arresting big shots!"

"Charles Bonner may be a big shot," Hugo told her, "but I have one thing he doesn't have. A wife! Poor Charles Bonner doesn't know what he's missing, not having a wife to nag him."

"Maybe he doesn't need a wife because he's smart enough to button up his own coat," Maggie Rose answered, buttoning Hugo's. She reached to kiss his cheek. Even though she stood on tiptoe, Hugo had to lean down to receive her kiss. He hugged her hard as she clung to him and said, "God watch over you, my darling."

Karl and his father left by the front door and walked in silence along Chestnut Street until they reached Center Street. Snowflakes the size of silver quarters skimmed beneath the lights of the streetlamps, as dense as moths on a summer night.

"Mayo Culley giveth, and Mayo Culley taketh away," Hugo mused as they clumped through the snow. "But you know, son, I haven't much enjoyed being chief of police. It bothers me to see the foreign men locked up for drunkenness. They only drink because they're lonesome for their women in the old country. So if I lose this job, I'll be pretty glad to get back in the mill."

Karl didn't answer, feeling certain that his father would never again be hired in the Canaan Works, or any other mill of the Carnegie Steel Company, if he arrested superintendent Charles Bonner.

"Here's a dollar, Karl," Hugo said, pressing a bill into Karl's hand. "It's your pay for being deputy tonight. No, I want you to take it," he insisted when Karl tried to refuse. "You'll earn it, going with me on this peculiar business."

When they reached the big iron gates at the bottom of the drive to the superintendent's mansion, Hugo pushed the latch, and the gate swung open. "Strange," Hugo said. "If there's such a big poker party going on inside, you'd think to find automobile tracks in the snow, or at least a lot of footprints. I'm not any great shakes as a detective, Karl, but it looks like just one set of footprints has gone inside here tonight."

"It's hard to tell, Pop," Karl answered. "The falling snow might have covered up the rest, if the men came early." But to Karl, too, on the way up the drive, only one nearly filled set of footprints was visible.

"Brush your coat off, son, and stomp the snow from your boots," Hugo told him at the mansion's tall carved door. "We don't want to track slush into this pretty house."

It was Mary Margaret Culley who answered their knock, dressed in her black maid's clothes with a white cap and apron. "Mr. Kerner!" she exclaimed, looking surprised to see them.

"Working late tonight, Mary Margaret?" Hugo asked her.

"Oh no. I stay here all the time now. Didn't Jame mention it?"

"He didn't. I would like to see Mr. Bonner, please." Hugo

spoke courteously, and Karl surprised himself by pulling off his cap out of politeness to Mary Margaret. She seemed changed: less awkward, less stooped, not as shy. Working at the general superintendent's mansion must agree with her, Karl thought.

"Mr. Bonner is in the drawing room," Mary Margaret told them. "Follow me, please."

She led them along a wide hallway, its wall hung with portraits. Karl recognized one of Andrew Carnegie. A curved stairway of dark, polished wood ascended from the center of the hall, but Mary Margaret passed the stairs and paused before an imposing double door of wood so dark it was almost black. She knocked softly.

"Yes?" From inside the room, a man's voice answered the knock.

Mary Margaret opened the door to step a little way into the drawing room. "Excuse me, Mr. Bonner. You have callers."

"All right, show them in."

Mary Margaret bobbed a curtsy before she turned to Hugo and Karl. "You may go in."

The room was not as large as Karl had expected, but he didn't take time to examine it because his attention was held by two men seated on either side of the fireplace. Charles Bonner had on a maroon velvet smoking jacket—Karl knew what it was because he'd seen one in a Hart Schaffner and Marx advertisement. Bonner looked somewhat exasperated, but Karl sensed that it was not because of the interruption.

Harry Ward sat in the chair opposite Bonner. Except for the narrowing of his eyes when Hugo and Karl appeared, his expression remained controlled.

"I don't believe I know you," Charles Bonner said to Hugo.

"I'm Hugo Kerner, police chief of the borough of Canaan. This is my son Karl."

"What can I do for you?" Bonner asked politely.

Hugo had removed his hat and held it in front of him. His hair was cropped short; he'd always worn it that way, shaved high above the ears in the Prussian style. In the light from the large chandelier overhead, Karl noticed how gray his father's hair had become, making Hugo look vulnerable as he stood before the two important men.

"Mr. Bonner," Hugo said, "earlier this evening I was told that a gambling party was going on in this house. I came to investigate, because gambling is illegal in the borough of Canaan, even in private homes."

Charles Bonner smiled, his thin face with the straight eyebrows and high-bridged nose losing some of its aloofness in the smile. "Chief Kerner, you can see there's no one here except myself and Mr. Ward. I assure you we are not gambling. We're discussing the election."

Hugo said, "I'm sorry, Mr. Bonner, but I'll have to inspect the premises."

A look of alarm crossed Bonner's face, but so quickly that Karl wasn't certain he'd seen it. "If you're sure it's absolutely necessary, I can tell the maid to show you around," Bonner answered.

"Necessary? Why would it be necessary?" Harry Ward blustered. "If Mr. Bonner says there's no gambling going on here, Kerner, his word should be good enough for you."

Charles Bonner had risen from his chair. He stared down at Harry Ward with evident distaste. "I don't need you to defend my interests, Ward," he said. "If someone has accused me of violating the law, I'd just as soon get the mistake cleared up. I'll go find the maid."

Harry Ward flushed, but remained silent. After Bonner left the room, Ward lolled back against the high leather armchair and said, "Looks like you're being a little overzealous in your duty, Kerner." His voice was noncommittal, but a tight trace of smile curved his lips.

"I'm performing my duty as I see it," Hugo replied stiffly.

Harry Ward bit the end off a cigar and spat it into a cuspidor. He took a long time lighting the cigar, to avoid saying more, Karl suspected.

"Karl," Hugo said quietly, "Mr. Bonner has been gone longer than he should have been just to call Mary Margaret. See if you can find where he is. I'll stay here in case he comes back."

Karl crossed the thick carpet and opened the library door, which Bonner had shut behind him.

Mary Margaret stood just outside the door as though she'd been trying to overhear what was going on inside—not as though she'd been summoned to show Hugo around the house. Karl expected her to look embarrassed because he'd caught her eavesdropping, but instead she looked worried.

"Where'd Mr. Bonner go?" he asked her.

She hesitated, then in a quick, jerky motion pointed to the staircase. "Up there."

Karl climbed the stairs, letting his fingers brush against the polished banister. Since he was wearing his rubber galoshes, his footfalls didn't clatter on the wooden steps. The top of the staircase opened onto another long hall decorated with portraits like the ones below, hanging between half a dozen closed doors that lined the hall. Karl was reluctant to start knocking on one door after another to locate Charles Bonner, so he stood, undecided, at the head of the stairs.

Almost immediately, a door at the far end of the hall opened, and Charles Bonner came out. Because he was turned, looking back into the room he'd just left, he didn't see Karl.

"Hurry," Bonner said to someone in the room. "Come down the back stairs and go to the gardener's cottage." He said it quietly, but his voice, accustomed to rising with authority, reached Karl.

Maybe there really is a poker party going on, Karl thought, but before he had a chance to start down the staircase to tell his father, a woman followed Charles Bonner out of the room. She wore a lacy nightdress, and held her head bent as she struggled to push her arms into the sleeves of a coat. Her long hair hung halfway down her back; she raised an arm to pull the hair free from her coat.

Charles Bonner had gone ahead of her and was already descending the back stairs. The woman stumbled, then bent to adjust one of her shoes; in her hurry she must have put them on improperly. As she straightened, she caught sight of Karl.

The woman was Yulyona Petrov.

For a long moment they stared at one another, Karl too startled to comprehend Yulyona's presence in the general superintendent's mansion. Yulyona's expression was unreadable in the dim light.

Charles Bonner's voice rose from the back stairwell. "What's keeping you, Yulie? Hurry!"

Yulyona turned to follow Bonner. Karl, still bewildered, made his way back to the library on the first floor, and had just entered it when Charles Bonner came in, directly behind him.

"Sorry to be so long. I couldn't find the maid," Bonner told Hugo. "But I'll take you through the house myself if you want."

"That won't be necessary, Charles," Harry Ward announced, belligerent again. "Chief Kerner, you've overstepped your authority, coming here to harass Canaan's most respected citizen. Whatever scheme you're trying to pull, forget it, because you're no longer chief of police. You're fired right now. In fact, you're damn lucky I'm firing you, because otherwise you could be tried for improper search and seizure."

"Hold on a minute, Ward," Charles Bonner interrupted. "I'd like to get to the bottom of this. Surely Kerner wouldn't have come here if someone hadn't given him false information. Please have a seat, Mr. Kerner, and we'll . . . "

Karl didn't hear the rest of Bonner's words, because at that moment the realization struck him. Upstairs were the bedrooms. Yulyona had been dressed in nightclothes. She and Charles Bonner must be . . . adulterers!

Yes, Karl knew what the word meant. He'd first heard it in catechism class when he was a little kid, but he hadn't understood it until Andy explained it later.

Yulyona! Doing that with Bonner!

Moving woodenly, Karl passed through the library door, which Bonner had left open. The men didn't notice him leave, and Mary Margaret was gone from the hall. Quietly opening the front door, he stepped into the snow and ran down the driveway, his hot cheeks growing wet from the snowflakes that struck them and melted.

Yulyona was a . . . a . . . His mind wouldn't allow him to

use the name his terrible hurt wanted him to use, a name he could easily have called the painted women he'd seen through the windows of Canaan's shadier taverns. Yet his mind wouldn't stop tormenting him with the image of Yulyona in the lacy nightdress, coming out of Charles Bonner's bedroom.

And Karl had loved her! He'd been willing to give his life to her, to let her make of him what she wanted. And all the time he'd been sitting in her classroom, longing for her to show him just one small sign of affection, she'd been doing . . . that . . . with Bonner.

Karl ran up Pine Alley as though trying to outrace his terrible discovery about her, barely able to hold back the cries that struggled to tear out of his chest. When he reached the woodshed he threw back the door and gasped, "Andy? You still here?"

"I was just getting ready to leave," Andy answered. "If I wait much longer, I'll miss the freight."

"I'm going with you," Karl cried.

3

All night long the mournful locomotive whistle shrieked through falling snow, giving voice to Karl's anguish.

After Karl's first refusal to explain the reason he was running away from Canaan, Andy hadn't pressed him for an answer. Andy was too occupied with his own gloom. At the end of a long line of gondolas filled with coal from the mines of West Virginia, they'd found one empty boxcar. As though the railroad had cooperated to make their escape easy, the boxcar door stood open just wide enough for the two of them to crawl inside.

Sleep was impossible. The boxcar, designed to haul heavy

loads, rode rough because it was empty. When Karl tried to lie down on the steel floor, he was bounced so hard he felt bruised. If he stood, his knees took such a jarring from the train's motion that they throbbed with spasms. Only squatting was barely tolerable, although his calf and thigh muscles grew sore and cramped.

His mental agony was worse than his physical discomfort. Through the hours of darkness, Karl was tormented with images of Yulyona, of Charles Bonner's hands on her in places Karl had never imagined touching her—not in his waking thoughts, at least, but only in the secrecy of dreams he couldn't control while he slept. He moaned out loud, the moans muffled by the clatter of the train as the night wore on, until thin lines of gray dawn showed around the edges of the boxcar door.

When the freight pulled in at Erie, Pennsylvania, in the middle of the following morning, the snowfall had stopped. The railroad yard shone white in the sunlight, its steel rails, bright as silver, curving in parallel lines from the flatness of the open country behind them to the loading docks on the shores of Lake Erie. After Andy and Karl had lowered themselves from the boxcar without bungling into a railroad detective, Andy led Karl along the tracks, looking for a place to buy food.

"There's a kid selling papers over there," Andy said. "We'll ask him where we can eat."

A scarf wrapped several times around the newsboy's neck hid his chin; his cheeks were chapped bright red and his fingers were blue. "Paper!" he yelled, although no one was near except Andy and Karl. "Read all about the election!"

"Hey, let me see that headline," Andy said, grabbing a paper from the boys hand. "Look at this, Karl. Woodrow Wilson won. Taft and Roosevelt split the Republican party, and the Democrats sneaked in. Well, what do you know about that! Isn't that something!"

It didn't matter in the least to Karl that Woodrow Wilson would be the next president. Nothing mattered, except the hurt inside him, which had grown so much worse it left no room for any other thoughts. Yulyona's face wouldn't leave him—Yulyona smiling, laughing as she danced with him, Yulyona wearing the nightgown . . .

"If you wanna read the paper, buy it!" the newsboy demanded. "I ain't the public library."

Andy handed back the paper and asked the kid, "Where can we get some breakfast?"

"Ain't no place around here, big spender," the kid jeered. "There's a greasy spoon down by the docks, but the guys that hang around there are real tough. They'll probably eat *you* for breakfast."

"Come on." Andy took Karl's arm and pulled him through the untracked snow.

At the docks, Andy forgot his hunger at the sight of an enormous steamship being unloaded. On one end of a bridge-like crane, a big steam shovel, shaped like an open clam shell, lowered its jaws into the hold of the ship and bit into tons of iron ore. Then the clam shell swung high above a hopper. It dropped the ore, which slid down chutes into waiting railroad cars.

"Look at the size of that ship!" Andy yelled. "It must be six hundred feet long."

"You got a good eye, kid. She's six hundred five feet overall and has a fifty-eight-foot beam. She's the *J. Pierpont Morgan*, christened after the millionaire of the same name."

The man who spoke to Andy was leaning against one of the steel girders that supported the steam-powered unloader. He was short and fat, with upper arms as round as hams. "You kids just get off a freight?" he asked, shouting to be heard above the racket of machinery and the crash of dumped ore.

Andy eyed the man with suspicion. "You a railroad cop?"

"Not me. I'm the cook on the *J. Pierpont Morgan,*" he answered. "I could tell you two come off a coal freight because you're both black from coal dirt. I used to ride the rails myself, when I was a kid like you."

"Say, mister, maybe you could tell us where to get something to eat," Andy hollered. "We're starved."

The man shifted against the girder. "Where're you two headin'?"

"No place special." Andy was doing all the talking. His dejection seemed to have disappeared in excitement over the sights of the loading dock, while Karl's depression grew worse, deepened by exhaustion.

"My name's Norris," the man said, shaking hands first with Andy and then with Karl. "Tell you what. After this ore gets unloaded, the *Morgan's* gonna get filled up with coal, then we'll take her across the lake to Detroit. If you fellas want to come along for the ride, I could use a little help in the galley, and the guys in the boiler room can always find work for an extra coal passer."

"Swell!" Andy replied. "I mean, what do you say, Karl?"

Karl shrugged. Let Andy make the decisions.

After they followed the cook on board the *Morgan,* he showed them where to wash up. Inside the galley, he let them polish off a plateful of cold ham and fried potatoes left over from the morning meal. Even after two cups of hot coffee Karl was so numb he could hardly function.

"You can stretch out over there in the corner where it's warm," Norris told them after Karl and Andy had washed a tub full of greasy dishes. "I'm going topside again. We won't leave port for another six hours or so, not till the coal's loaded." Norris was barely out the galley door before Karl lay on the floor and fell into a heavy sleep.

He wakened an hour later because Andy was punching his shoulder. "Karl, get up," Andy told him. "You got to see this. They're loading the coal, and it's the dangdest thing."

Karl heard the thunder of coal dropping into the ship's hold–it was so loud he wondered how he'd slept through it. Shaking his head to clear away the grogginess, he followed Andy up a flight of stairs. They emerged at the ship's bow, on the deck beneath the pilot house. Karl hadn't paid attention earlier to the size of the *Morgan,* but now he stared along her length to the silver-painted smokestack rising from the stern, a tenth of a mile away.

During the hour that Karl had slept, the *Morgan* had moved to a different dock from the one where Andy and Karl boarded. She floated beneath a steel trestle that rose alongside her to a height of seventy feet and stretched to three times the length of the ship. On top of the trestle stood the line of gondola cars from the freight train they'd hopped in Canaan; Karl could read the P and LE markings on the sides. The bottoms of a dozen of the gondolas had been opened to spill coal from the cars into chutes that reached down into the ship's hold. The coal made such a racket cascading down the chutes–about as loud as three simultaneous thunderstorms–that Karl couldn't hear Andy, even when he yelled. So Andy just pointed to the deepening mounds of coal, widening his eyes to show his fascination.

Drawn by the fury of the falling coal, Karl moved to the edge of the deck overlooking the hold. He stared spellbound as the mounds of coal rose out of their black dust, reaching toward him. No railing barricaded the deck from the hold—a person could stand too close to the edge and fall twenty feet, be smothered and crushed beneath tons of unyielding blackness. The explosion of sound as the coal crashed into the hold drove thought from his mind, dulled his pain, hypnotized him. He leaned forward, balancing himself above the swelling mountain of coal, lulled by the thought-numbing roar.

Andy's arms encircled Karl, pulled him backward. "Are you crazy?" Andy yelled, his mouth against Karl's ear. "You could get killed standing here. What's the matter with you?"

Karl frowned at Andy. If he'd been able to feel anything except the hurt that filled him, he'd have felt anger that Andy had pulled him away from oblivion, back to the remembrance of why he hurt so much. Not answering, he let Andy lead him down to the galley.

That evening Karl washed dishes and scrubbed all the pots and pans while Norris sat and played a harmonica. As Karl wiped off the tables in the dining room, he felt the ship rock as it moved into the harbor.

"I'm gonna turn in now," Norris told him. "You can sleep in the galley where you slept this afternoon. Your friend will bunk down in the boiler room, if the stokers let him get any sleep at all. You got the soft job. Andy's gonna work his butt off."

"Does the ship always sway this much?" Karl asked, bracing himself against a table to keep his balance.

"So you *can* talk. I was starting to think you couldn't say anything but 'yep' and 'nope.' The lake's a little choppy to-night," Norris said to answer Karl's question, "what sailors call a nasty bit of slop. Nothing the *Morgan* can't handle, though. By morning we'll be steaming up the channel to Detroit. You and your pal can leave ship after you finish cleaning the galley."

When Norris went to bed, Karl lay on the galley floor next to the still-warm ovens, but the ship's motion rolled him from side to side. After two hours, during which the rocking grew much worse, he gave up trying to sleep and climbed the stairs to the deck.

Wind hit him with such force it nearly knocked him back-ward down the stairs. The water, instead of being "a little choppy," rose in twenty-foot crests that burst against the ship's hull, sending spumes of spray across the deck. Karl had never before been on board a ship, and he'd certainly never seen anything as awesome as the house-high waves that roared toward the *J. Pierpont Morgan.* Wind howled, water crashed, the ship cracked and groaned in an explosion of noises.

Karl leaned against the ship's railing, again thinking how easy it would be to let himself go, to fall into destruction. If a wave pulled him overboard, tons of water would crush him just as heavily as the coal in the hold would have crushed him that afternoon, and this time Andy wasn't there to pull him back.

Half a year earlier, the great ship *Titanic* had gone down in the North Atlantic, dragging hundreds of people to their deaths. Did it matter to them, Karl wondered. Were any of them already crushed inside, as he was, so that the weight of the ocean was no heavier than the pain they already carried?

Were any of them already cold and dead inside, so that the icy waters couldn't hurt them further, but only put an end to the pain?

A wave higher than the rest burst against the ship and knocked Karl to the deck, splashing the boards slick. As he slid toward the edge, instinct made him fling his arms and legs around a post supporting the rail. The wave sucked backward, ripping a sob from Karl's chest, releasing his anguish. He clung to the post as the storm lashed at his tears and his cries for Yulyona.

4

"Leave your cap and coat under the bush here, Karl," Wabash Sam told him. "They'll be safe till we come out."

Eight days before, the *J. Pierpont Morgan* had steamed into Detroit harbor, after the night of the wild storm Norris said was " . . . nothing much to speak of; you ought to see it when we have real weather!"

Their first day in Detroit, Karl and Andy had ridden a streetcar out Woodward Avenue to Highland Park. Andy had decided they would apply for jobs in the Ford automobile factory, and Karl went along because it seemed easiest to let Andy worry about what happened to them. Karl didn't much care.

When they learned Ford wasn't hiring, they walked the six miles back to the waterfront to save carfare. Late that evening, because Andy didn't want to spend money on a boardinghouse room, they joined a gang of hoboes beneath a stone overpass of the Michigan Central Railroad.

The friendly hoboes fed them, and one, Wabash Sam, took a particular interest in Karl. "You're just what I've been lookin'

for, kid," Sam had told him. "You come along with me tomorrow. Workin' together, you and me can have a soft winter.

"What kind of work?" Karl asked.

"Nice and easy." Beside the sporadic warmth of the hobo
campfire, which cast ragged shadows on the stones of the
overpass, Wabash Sam coached Karl in the role he'd have to
play.

The scam was simple. They tried it the next day. Walking
through Detroit's fashionable neighborhoods, they knocked
on the back doors of a series of imposing homes, one after the
other. When a door was opened, usually by an Irish kitchen
maid, Wabash Sam would go into a spiel guaranteed to
squeeze sympathy from the woman's gullible heart.

He was the father of seven children, Sam would tell her,
his voice catching on a sob. He was out of work, his wife was
dreadful sick, the whole family faced starvation, and his oldest son, Karl, had been touched with lung fever.

At this point Karl was supposed to cough convincingly,
his only part in the drama. Sam would then ask whether the
woman could spare a bite of food, and perhaps some discarded clothing to shield poor Karl from the bitterness of the
Detroit winter.

On their first day together, they collected two jackets, an
overcoat, three hats, a scarf, and a woolen stocking cap, all of
which Sam sold to a secondhand clothing dealer. In addition,
they'd been fed so much good food that Karl had trouble swal-
lowing the last of it.

"It's them baby-blue eyes of yours," Sam chortled. "When
I first caught sight of you, I knew you'd do perfect. You got
that heartbroken look that makes them greenhorn women
want to mother you."

Karl didn't answer. The begging humiliated him, but the numbness inside him sapped his energy so that he couldn't bother to oppose Wabash Sam. He was also unable to resist his body's demand for food, which the scam supplied, and which neither Karl nor Andy had been able to supply for themselves.

Andy had been unsuccessful in finding honest work. He spent his days with a group of unemployed steelworkers who got meals from a charity kitchen, and when he returned to the hobo jungle at night, his talk was full of the things he was learning from the men.

"They really know a whole lot about labor and industry and the American economic system," Andy enthused.

That didn't interest Karl—he paid hardly any attention to the things Andy said. Nothing interested him. If Andy hadn't come back to the bridge each night, pushing Karl closer to the fire, finding him a pile of rags to sleep on inside the hobo shanty, as far as possible from the crack-ridden walls, Karl would have grown sick from exposure. Mindlessly, he let Andy watch over him at night, let Wabash Sam use him during the days.

So on that Friday morning, a week after Karl had joined Wabash Sam in their fraudulent scheme, Sam led him up the drive toward the most luxurious house they'd yet approached.

Because a crumb of bread from a handout he'd received at the last house was lodged in Karl's throat, his cough was genuine for a change. Even before Sam began to con her, the kitchen maid who opened the door gazed at Karl with sympathy. Her broad Irish face shone red from the heat of the cookstove; her eyes had their own warmth.

"The poor dear lad," she commiserated when Sam had

finished his speech. "Let you bring him inside, then, out of the cold. God's hand is in this, I'm sure, for this very day the master told me to get rid of a coat and hat he wants no longer. He was for givin' them to the stableboy, but they're far too grand for the likes of that loafer. And they'll fit your poor son much better."

She'd crossed the room to return holding the coat and a narrow-brimmed homburg. "Do you know why the master don't want these no more?" she asked, raising the garments, which looked brand-new. Even before she answered her own question, her laughter rang out in such infectious, full-throated merriment that it brushed a bit of warmth against the coldness inside Karl, made him feel a touch of interest.

"Because . . . ," the woman gasped, her eyes teary with mirth, " . . . while he had them on outside, a pigeon dropped a load on him! I cleaned them good so you'd never tell, but the master . . . !" She was laughing so hard she could hardly go on. " . . . the divil himself couldn't make him put them on again, he's that finicky."

Dabbing her eyes with her apron, she said, "God forgive me for hooting about the gent that pays me wages. Here, lad, try them on, unless a little pigeon muck offends yourself as well. No, truly, it's all cleaned off," she said, still giggly.

She held the overcoat so that Karl could slip his arms through the sleeves. It fit as though it had been cut to his body by a fine tailor.

"Aren't you the great wonder!" she said, stepping back to admire Karl.

The overcoat was charcoal gray, with a black velvet collar. Before Karl buttoned it, he read the label inside—The House of Kuppenheimer, Chicago. He ran his hands over his chest, feeling the soft strength of wool finer than he'd ever before touched. Wabash Sam's eyes brightened at the thought of the price he could get for the overcoat from the secondhand dealer.

"Here, let me put the hat on you," the woman said. "Glory be, that fits, too! You look like a proper nob. God bless you, lad, and I'm prayin' the coat helps your lungs improve. You remind me of my own dear baby brother back home in County Cork."

Her genuine concern stirred a response in Karl. He reached for her hand and held it tightly. "God bless you too," he said. "You're a kind woman."

"Go along wit' yez," she answered shyly, her face even redder than it had been when they entered.

Karl had to drop her hand then and hurry through the door, because he felt like such a heel for deceiving her.

Wabash Sam gloated all the way down the drive, but silently. When they reached the bush where Karl had hidden his own cap and coat, far beyond hearing of anyone in the house, Sam let out a whoop. "Do you know how much I can get for that fancy overcoat?" he asked, smacking Karl on the back. "Twenty simoleons, at least! That was some act you put on back there. 'You're such a kind woman,'" Sam mimicked.

"Shut your face," Karl growled.

"Ah, come on, kid, don't go gettin' soft on me. We got a good thing goin' here. Them pig-Irish broads are too stupid to know when they're bein' bamboozled. . . ."

Sam choked on his next words because Karl had slammed him against a high brick wall. Enraged, Karl shouted, "My mother came from Ireland. She worked as a maid for six years. Worked hard! My father works hard too. They don't go around lying and cheating people to get handouts."

It was the longest string of words Karl had spoken since he left Canaan, and it felt good to get them out. In letting them explode from his mouth, it was as if he'd opened the way for his feelings to break loose from the desolate place where they'd been tormenting him.

Releasing Sam, he cried, "What am I doing here?" The question was to himself, not Sam. "I've got a good home waiting for me. I'd be crazy to keep on doing this."

He rolled up his old overcoat and stalked down Jefferson Street, with Sam scurrying after him. "Where are you going?" Sam cried. "Take off that new coat and put your old one back on. Listen, if I get ... uh ... ten bucks for that overcoat, I'll give you a whole dollar. You can even keep the homburg hat."

Karl didn't bother to answer. Wabash Sam, who was running to keep up because his legs were much shorter than Karl's, kept plucking Karl's sleeve from behind. "Come on, kid, give me the coat. It belongs to me. I thought up this whole scheme. Give me the coat!"

"No!" Karl whirled so quickly that Sam ran into him. "I've been shaming myself for you for a whole week, and you never gave me a single dime from all the stuff you pawned. You didn't even have to feed me, because those pig Irish, as you call them, took pity on us and gave us food. So I'm keeping this coat and hat that *Irish* woman wanted me to have. She has more ... decency! ... in her little fingernail than you have in your whole filthy body."

"Don't get sore. You can keep the coat," Sam answered meekly. "Only, let's not gum up the works on this little operation we're running."

"Go fall on your face," Karl told him. "I'm going home."

Karl walked rapidly along Jefferson Street toward the waterfront, not turning back to see whether Sam was following. He planned to search the docks for the *J. Pierpont Morgan.* If she was in port, he'd ask Norris if he could work for passage back to Erie. Before he did any of that, though, he'd have to find Andy and tell him he was heading for home. Maybe by now Andy would be ready to return to Canaan too.

At the hobo jungle under the stone overpass, Karl learned that Andy had left a message for him. Jake the Butcher, a gentle hobo with rheumy eyes, told Karl, "Your pal said you was to meet him at seven o'clock tonight in the Fort Street Union Depot. Say, where'd you get them clothes? You look like a real swell."

"The Fort Street Union Depot?" Karl asked. "Where's that?"

"On Fort Street, where do you think? Fort and Third."

"Thanks, Jake. I need to get passage on a steamship across the lake. Do you know if the *J. Pierpont Morgan* is docked here?"

"Too late, sonny," Jake told him. "All the lake vessels stopped runnin' yesterday, and they won't start again till spring. Too much ice in Lake Erie already. When the ice gets thick, the ships tie up for winter."

Karl grimaced. "Shoot! That means I'll have to ride the rails all the way home." After receiving directions from Jake on how to reach Union Depot, Karl left the hobo jungle, glad he'd never have to spend another night there. The hoboes had been kind and generous, but at night the shack filled with their sleeping bodies smelled rank, and the badly nailed boards couldn't keep out the cold.

Union Depot stood only a few blocks from the waterfront. It looked like a fortress, with a square corner tower topped by two clocks at right angles, so that people could read the time from either Fort Street or Third. Both clocks pointed to four-thirty—Karl would have a long wait for Andy.

Inside the depot, Karl peered into trash cans until he found discarded brown wrapping paper in one, and a length of string in another. He wrapped and tied his old overcoat and cap together, carrying the bundle with him when he went into the men's room.

Seeing his reflection in a mirror for the first time in a week and a half, Karl was horrified at how dirty he looked. In Canaan, he'd grown used to the nightly showers he'd taken for Yulyona's benefit. Since he left Canaan, he'd neither washed his body nor changed his clothes, and the sight of his dirtiness disgusted him.

Karl scrubbed his face and hands in the men's room sink and washed his hair, drying it on a roller towel. He flattened the damp hair with his palms before putting the homburg back on his head.

The depot's waiting room was warm, and Karl dozed on a bench, waking every few minutes to look at the clock. Andy appeared at exactly seven.

"Holy gee, you look like you won the Irish sweepstakes," Andy exclaimed when he saw Karl. "Where'd you get the nifty outfit?"

"Not from the Irish sweepstakes—from an Irish samaritan," Karl told him.

"Am I hearing you right?" Andy asked, breaking into a grin. "Was that a feeble attempt at a joke? It sounds like you're coming out of the black mopes you've been in ever since we left Canaan."

"I think I am," Karl answered. "I guess the lady who gave

me the new clothes helped me snap out of it. Do I look good?"

"Classy! Except your shirt's pretty filthy, and you don't have a necktie. Here, take my scarf and put it under your coat to hide the shirt. Go on, take it. I won't need it. I have a train ticket, so I'm gonna ride the coach this time, not a boxcar."

"Andy! You're going home too? I just decided to go back to Canaan myself."

Andy sank onto the bench beside Karl. He seemed taut with excitement. "I'm not going to Canaan. I'm going to Gary, Indiana. I planned to figure out some way to take you with me, but if you're going home, that's a hell of a lot better. For you, I mean. I'll still go to Gary."

"Why Gary?" Karl asked.

"Listen," Andy said, "I have a lot to talk to you about, and there isn't much time. I haven't eaten all day, but I don't want to go back to the Salvation Army kitchen because we won't be able to talk there. Let's go to Mike Quinn's saloon around the corner. I have enough money to buy a beer for each of us so we can eat the free lunch."

Andy wouldn't explain any more until the two of them stood at the bar in the saloon. Because most of the patrons had gone home for supper, Karl had room to set his bundle on the bar's polished counter. The bored bartender didn't seem to mind that Karl and Andy helped themselves to hardboiled eggs, pickles, and pretzels.

"Tell me why you're going to Gary," Karl demanded after they'd been served their beers.

"To organize a union."

"A union! Andy, you don't know anything about organizing a union," Karl said, twisting around to face him.

"That's why I'm going to Gary. To learn. I've already learned a lot about unions, talking to those steelworkers for the past week. Those guys are out of work because they got kicked out of the steel plants around here for union activity. Literally kicked out. On their butts."

"So why do they want to drag you into that kind of trouble?"

Andy fussed while removing his cap, pushing back his hair to try to conceal the pride in his face. "They think I'm smart. They want me to join them in union work because I've got a good head for details, they said."

"Oh yeah?" Karl challenged. "Do you know what the cops do to union agitators? You could get your good head for details busted in with a club."

"Not agitators, Karl. Organizers. And if my head gets busted, it'll be for a good cause."

Speaking quietly, so the bartender wouldn't hear, Karl asked, "Are you turning into an anarchist?"

"They're not the same thing, Karl—anarchists and union organizers." Andy leaned forward in his earnestness, his eyes troubled by Karl's question. "Too many people think unions mean anarchy, but they don't. The whole steel industry's got to be unionized, if people like me are ever gonna get decent jobs." Andy toyed with his beer mug, nudging it in circles to spread the wetness beneath it. "I'm ashamed to admit this, but before I met those men, I was planning to change my name. From Andrej Stulak to Andrew Steel." He smiled wryly. "That's Andrew, after Carnegie, and Steel for our noble industry. Thank God I heard those union men talking, or I might have sold my heritage for a mess of—crap!"

"You wouldn't have been the first one," Karl murmured.

"Yeah. Well, unions will put an end to all that. When the steel industry gets organized, Slovaks like me will be as good as anyone else in the mills. Look at us, Karl," Andy said suddenly, pointing to the mirror over the bar. "We look like a mural of a workingman and an industrialist."

Quinn's Saloon was illuminated by old-fashioned gas lamps. Their soft glow burnished the waves in Andy's blond hair. His rough overcoat, reflected in the glass, had grimed to dingy gray, and had lost a top button. Andy's hands circling the beer mug looked broad, strong, and soiled.

Karl had not removed the homburg; its brim shadowed his face, so that his highlighted jawline seemed aristocratic. The Kuppenheimer overcoat lay smoothly against his shoulders, and the scarf, which he'd put on only to hide his dirty shirt collar, lent him elegance.

"Did you notice the bartender didn't ask if we were old enough to drink?" Karl mentioned. "Speaking of age, what's today's date?"

"November fifteenth."

"Then I'll be home for my birthday. It's the twentieth." Karl finished the beer and wiped foam from his lip. "I'm gonna hate like the devil to leave you, Andy, but I'm glad I'll be home on time. Kathleen's birthday was tough for my mom."

"God only knows when I'll get back to Canaan," Andy said. "If things go right for me, maybe someday I can go back there and organize a union. Anyway, since we won't be together on your birthday, let me buy you one more beer to celebrate."

Andy raised his hand to signal for another beer, then spun a dime down the length of the counter to the bartender. He said to Karl, "You know, you never did tell me why you left Canaan. Want to tell me now?"

Catching the full mug the bartender slid to him, Karl answered, "I never should have gone at all. Things happened too fast, before I had a chance to think straight. You were leaving, the train pulled in right on time—everything made it easy for me to run from what hurt me, so I ran. Because I was hurting bad."

Andy waited, his silence indicating that he was willing to listen if Karl wanted to talk. Karl decided to tell the truth. As Andy had said, only God knew when they'd be together again.

"It was because of Yulyona Petrov," he admitted. "I was in love with her. I guess I still am. That night, before you and I left, Pop took me with him to the general superintendent's mansion. I saw Yulyona there, coming out of a bedroom, wearing a nightgown."

One side of Andy's mouth curved in a sympathetic grin. "So now you know too," he said. "It's supposed to be a secret, but I guess you won't tell anyone." Andy took a slow sip of beer, then added, "I only know myself because my sister Veronica was a bridesmaid."

Karl stared at him, bewildered. "Bridesmaid? What are you talking about?"

"About Charles Bonner and Yulyona getting married last June. They're keeping it a secret, because Yulyona wants to teach for at least a year. You know, she worked really hard to get her education, and married women aren't allowed to teach."

Karl was stunned. "They're married?"

"Sure. What did you think? Oh . . . I get it. You thought . . ." Andy started to laugh. "Not Yulyona! She's as straight as they come."

Karl leaned heavily against the bar, not even noticing that he'd spilled beer over his fingers. He felt immensely relieved, although he couldn't explain to himself why he should be relieved to discover that Yulyona was married. It made her even less accessible to him than she'd have been otherwise. But at least he now knew that she was an honorable woman, not Charles Bonner's mistress, and that made his loss of her easier to bear. He sighed deeply, then shook his head. "Lord! Did I make a fool of myself, running away from Canaan. I wonder what she thought of me."

"She'll probably let you know when you get back," Andy commented, "Yulyona isn't shy about telling people what she . . . "

"One thing I can't figure out," Karl interrupted, still engrossed in the revelation about Yulyona. "Why would she marry the general superintendent of the Canaan Works, considering the way she feels about steel mills?"

"I don't know. They fell in love, I guess," Andy replied. "Politics isn't the only thing that makes strange bedfellows. Love does too."

Karl grunted, figuring that with all of Andy's reading, he probably knew more about love than Karl did. "So Mary Margaret knew they were married, because she works there," Karl said. "That's why she looked so worried when I went up the stairs—she was afraid I'd learn the secret. Boy, I'm sure glad you told me before I went home. It makes me feel a lot better about . . . about everything."

Andy said, "I'm glad you're finally out of the dumps, pal. You know, the way you've been acting since we left Canaan, I should have guessed it was something like that that made you feel so low."

"Why?" Karl asked.

"Because for the past ten days you've acted the way your mother did after Kurt and Kara died. You and your mother—you both love people so hard that you hit absolute bottom when you lose someone."

Karl's breath caught; he was stunned by Andy's observation. He had to wait a moment, give his mind time to recover from the impact, before he could decide whether what Andy said was true. He stared into his beer mug without seeing it. "I'm not sure . . . ," he began slowly, " . . . if I'm really like that. Maybe I am. But I don't know if my mom's that way so much anymore. She got over Kathleen's marriage pretty quick, didn't she?"

"That's because she hasn't really lost Kathleen," Andy replied. "Your mother still sees her a couple of times a week." Andy slid his arm around Karl's neck. "Hey, I didn't mean to hurt your feelings. I think you've done a swell job of pulling yourself out of this slump, and all on your own. I wish we had more time to talk about all this, but my train leaves in fifteen minutes."

Karl turned distressed eyes on Andy. Maybe it was true what Andy had said, about Karl not being able to handle losing people. He certainly didn't want Andy to go, now that the moment had arrived.

With his arm still around Karl's neck, Andy said, "Listen, I'm gonna give you three bucks out of the ten the steelworkers gave me. I only wish I could spare more, but I have to get to Gary and find a room. Use the money to buy a ticket for as far as it will take you. You look too spiffy to ride in a boxcar."

"Andy, I'm not taking your money," Karl protested. "You'll need it to live on."

Andy's arm tightened almost painfully around Karl. "If I was J. Pierpont Morgan, I'd buy you a whole goddang railroad to ride home on. Take the money and take care of yourself. You're the best friend I'll ever have." After a final squeeze, Andy released Karl and ran out of the saloon, leaving three silver dollars on the counter.

5

The train didn't stop or even slow down in Canaan, but chugged through the town at forty miles an hour. When the freight approached Center Street hill, Karl threw his bundle out the boxcar door and jumped after it, rolling as he hit the cinders alongside the tracks. The impact tore the knees from his pants and imbedded cinders in his hands, but he ignored the pain to search in the dark until he found his package. It held the Kuppenheimer coat and the homburg hat.

Three dollars had bought Karl a passenger ticket to Toledo, Ohio, with a dime left over to tip the porter. In the Toledo railroad yard, he'd waited for hours to find an unlocked boxcar on a train headed east. The trip had been brutal. From Cleveland to Pittsburgh he'd stood on the coupling between two fast-moving freight cars, one hand clinging to a ladder on the car ahead of him, the other arm pressing the bundle against his face to shield his eyes from cinders and his face from cold.

Karl was overjoyed to reach Canaan again. Even with its dirt, its pall of smoke that stung his nose and his lungs, its screech of steel mills in what would have been the silent hours of night anywhere else, Canaan was Karl's home, the place he wanted to spend his life. When he came to his gate on Pine Alley, wind momentarily cleft the smoky skies, so that moonlight made the Kerner house look like the flat backdrop of a stage set. Only more beautiful, and real.

He opened the kitchen door—they never locked it—and turned on the inside lights. Seven loaves of bread stood in a row on the table. Maggie Rose had evidently baked that evening, and set out the loaves to cool. Karl was so starved he wolfed down a whole loaf and half of another. And he was filthy, too disheveled to present himself to his parents as the prodigal son returned. He would rest for a little while on the parlor couch before cleaning himself to face Hugo and Maggie Rose after they awakened in the morning.

For hours his troubled dreams reenacted the lurch of a freight train, its racket. Then the pressure of a hand grew heavy on his shoulder—even in his sleep, Karl knew the hand expressed affection. He struggled to come awake. In the dim light from a parlor lamp, he saw his father's shape bent over him.

"Well, son," Hugo said, and his voice held only kindness, "what did you think of the world?"

6

On the morning of his sixteenth birthday, Karl woke up because Henry was sitting on his chest.

"Happy birthday," Henry said. "When are you going to play with me? All you do is sleep since you got home."

"No," Karl corrected him, "since I came home, all I've done is eat, sleep, and soak myself in the wooden tub. But finally I'm clean, full, and rested. So I'll play with you." He flipped Henry over onto the mattress and wrestled with him, taking pleasure in the little boy's squeals of delight.

Later he sent Henry downstairs with a message for their

mother that Karl would be down as soon as he'd dressed. He was hoping Maggie Rose would make pancakes for his birthday breakfast, since that was his favorite.

When he reached the kitchen, Maggie Rose stacked pancakes on a plate for him, saying, "So you finally got out of bed? I was ready to go upstairs and give you what Paddy gave the drum. Happy birthday, darlin'. I made enough batter for twice this many pancakes, so eat your fill. Henry already had his."

"Thanks, Mom. They look great. They *taste* great," Karl said, sampling them.

"I wanted to put a candle on your pancakes," Henry told Karl, "but Mom wouldn't let me."

"We'll save that for tonight—supper will be at six-thirty. That should give your pop just enough time to get washed up from the mill," Maggie Rose said. "Kathleen and Jame are coming too."

As Karl ate his breakfast, he reflected on his homecoming. His mother had been ecstatic to see him, and hadn't been as distraught over his disappearance as Karl had feared. "At first I was nearly destroyed," she told him, "but then, after we learned Andy was gone too, your father said that the two of you had likely gone off on a schoolboy adventure. Pop said it wouldn't last long—that you'd come home after you'd missed enough meals. And he was right."

Karl let his parents think that. He'd told the Stulaks that Andy had gone on to Gary to find work, and would probably write them before too long.

Karl's biggest surprise had been the news that superintendent Charles Bonner himself had rehired Hugo, and even promoted him to foreman on the open hearth. If the borough of Canaan couldn't appreciate an honest man, Hugo quoted Bonner as saying, the steel works could. According to Hugo, Charles Bonner suspected that Ward had tried to pull a fast one on Hugo, although Harry Ward was too crafty a politician to be caught in any shady dealings.

"I can't hold another bite," Karl said, pushing away his plate. "Mom, can I have a quarter for a haircut? I'd like to look nice for my birthday party."

"I'll give you thirty-five cents," she answered. "Get a shave, too. Your face looks whiskery."

"It does?" Karl hurried across the kitchen to stare into the mirror above the sink. "It does!" He twisted his face from side to side, impressed by the few coarse hairs that stuck out beneath his sideburns. "Tell you what, Mom. Give me an extra nickel, and I'll get a shoeshine too. I have a couple of important errands to take care of this afternoon."

Maggie Rose nodded, not asking what the errands were. The events of the past two months had taught her caution in dealing with her grown-up children. "Just be home on time for supper," she told him.

7

At four-thirty that afternoon Karl climbed the driveway to the general superintendent's mansion. Beneath the homburg, his hair was neatly trimmed. Beneath the Kuppenheimer overcoat, he wore his good suit. Inside his skin, his vital organs felt pressed together, like steel being forged into a difficult shape. He intended to call on Yulyona, and he didn't know what the encounter would do to him.

Mary Margaret answered his knock, her face lighting when she saw him. "Karl! Jame told me you'd returned home."

"I'd like to see Mrs. Bonner," he said.

Her smile faded as apprehension returned to her eyes. "You must be mistaken. There's no Mrs . . . ."

"It's all right, Mary Margaret. I know about it. Andy told me." She searched his face, then moved from the door to let him enter. "I'll go tell her you're here," she said. "Mrs. Bonner will be willing to receive you, most likely. She was considerably distressed when she learned you'd left Canaan."

Karl hid his astonishment at Mary Margaret's polished speech. She not only sounded far more cultivated than any of the rough-spoken Culleys ever had, she looked stylish, even in her maid's uniform. Her red-gold hair, the same color as Jame's, no longer frizzed, but was swept upward into smooth curls underneath the white cap. She could look people in the eye now, and speak to them without a tremor in her voice. Yulyona, the dedicated teacher, must have taken Mary Margaret in hand and found her to be an avid pupil.

"May I take your hat?" she asked.

"Uh . . . no, I'd like to keep it with me. I'll just hold it in my hand. Would that be all right?"

"Certainly. Please wait here. I'll announce you."

Mary Margaret moved gracefully down the hall—even her posture had improved. But Karl was too nervous to think about her. His heart thudded in anticipation of seeing Yulyona.

"Mrs. Bonner requests that you join her in the drawing room," Mary Margaret said when she returned. "She has already ordered tea. Please go in through the last door."

Inside the door, Yulyona waited for him with her hands outstretched. "I'm so glad you've come, Karl. Heavens! How could you have matured so much in just two weeks? But then, today is your sixteenth birthday, isn't it? Please take off that imposing coat—just throw it across the piano bench. Then come sit with me for a while."

She indicated a velvet-upholstered wing chair; Karl sank into it, glad to get off his feet because the impact of her beauty weakened him. She wore a deep-rose dress that heightened the color of her skin, the warmth of her eyes. Her long neck was sheathed in the lace-and-rose cloth of the high-collared dress, making her face look like a flower on a slender stem. Winter sunlight reached through the windows to gild her hair.

Almost immediately Mary Margaret came in with a tea tray. Yulyona hurried across the room, saying, "Let me help you with that—it's heavy. Set it on this table next to Karl. Would you like to have a cup of tea with us, Mary Margaret?"

The girl smiled her thanks, but shook her head. On the way out, she picked up Karl's coat and hat from the piano bench and took them with her.

"Lemon? Cream?" Yulyona asked, pouring the tea. "Have one of these cakes, Karl. I just got home from school, so I'm famished."

"Thank you." He held the teacup carefully—it was much smaller than the mugs they used at home. His fingers shook.

"I want to . . . ," he began, but at the same instant Yulyona said, "Karl, have you . . . ?"

She smiled. "You go first."

"I mainly came to tell you that I haven't said a word to anyone about your marriage." Mainly that, but mostly to see her one more time.

She answered, "I didn't suppose for a moment that you

would have told anyone. In fact, I was so confident I could trust you that I've never even mentioned to my husband that you saw me in the hall."

Karl was relieved to hear that. Until then, a shadow of suspicion had nagged him that Hugo might have been offered the mill job as an unnecessary bribe to keep him silent. "My father doesn't know anything about it either," he said. "The only person I told was Andy, and he already knew."

He sipped the tea; its warmth turned to heat inside him when Yulyona reached across the table between them, gently touching his hand. She gazed at him so directly that he was forced to look directly back, was unable to do anything except meet her eyes. "Karl," she asked, "why did you leave Canaan that night?"

He was proud that he could keep his gaze so steady. He even managed to smile a little. "Andy and I had planned it for a long time," he said. "It was just a schoolboy adventure." The teacup in his fingers rattled against its saucer; he pushed on it to quiet it.

Yulyona looked grave—maybe she doubted him—but all she said was, "Why don't you try some of these sandwiches? We have an English cook, and if I don't eat everything on the tea tray, he gets out of sorts. Usually Mary Margaret helps me."

She heaped his plate with small sandwiches cut into circles and triangles, filled with cream cheese and cucumbers. Although Karl was impressed that the cook could find cucumbers at that time of year, he didn't much like the taste of the sandwiches. He ate them, though, slowly, because he knew Yulyona would soon ask him another question, and his answer was going to displease her.

The question came sooner than he'd hoped. "Now that

you're sixteen," she asked, "what are your plans? Will you come back to school?"

Karl took a deep breath. "This afternoon I applied at the employment office of the Canaan Works. Tomorrow I start to work in the rail mill. No, wait!" he said, raising his hand. "Don't look disappointed until I have a chance to explain."

He folded his napkin and leaned forward, elbows on his knees, his hands clamped together to keep them steady. "Andy and I have always done a lot of talking," he said. "Andy is the smartest person I know—except you—and he told me that the reason men don't get ahead in the steel mills is because they never learn anything except their own jobs. A blast furnace man knows furnaces—that's all. A rolling mill man only knows about rolling billets. Nobody bothers to learn the overall process, from ore to steel. So that's what I'm going to do—learn everything. And the best place to do that is in the mill."

"You make it sound entirely too simplistic," she said. "It will be impossible for you to . . . "

"I'm young," he interrupted. "I'll spend a year in one part of the mill and then transfer to the next. And I'll study. Right there in the mill I ought to be able to understand books about steelmaking a lot better than college boys in their classrooms."

Almost before he'd finished speaking she answered, "You'll find that those college men will be promoted much more rapidly than you will."

"Maybe so," Karl answered, trying to counter her quick objections, "but I still want to try it my way. If it doesn't work, I can always try it another way. Miss . . . I mean, Mrs. Bonner, I'll never be a superintendent like your husband—I just don't have that kind of brains. But I think I can become a manager.

And when I do, I'll pay attention to the union men about ways to improve conditions in the mill."

"That's an admirable ambition," Yulyona said, her chin firming obstinately. "And you'd have a far greater chance of realizing it if you finished high school."

Karl leaned back in his chair, stung because she wouldn't listen to him, wouldn't concede even a little bit that it might be possible for him to achieve things in his own way. "I've already made up my mind," he said stiffly.

She jerked her napkin through its ring in swift, hard tugs. After a moment she said, "You'll have to forgive me if I sound unhappy. It's just . . . I almost won, didn't I? If you hadn't seen me in this house that night, you would have stayed in school."

Karl sucked in his breath. So she was going to cut through the pretense! Well, he could be truthful too. "Yes, if it hadn't been for that night, I probably would have finished high school. But for the wrong reasons."

Her voice rose as she hurled back, "For whatever reason you remained in school, it would have been to your advantage! It isn't fair that you're leaving simply because of an unfortunate . . . "

"Not fair!" he cried. "Who's been fair? Even though you were a married woman, you went to Veronica's wedding and danced with me. You made me believe . . . that night . . . that you liked me. Was that fair?"

"To whom? To my husband? Or to you?" Her eyes flashed—Karl was afraid he'd gone too far. "I went to Veronica's wedding because she's my dear friend," Yulyona declared. "I danced because I love to dance. Would you rather I'd refused to dance with you? Of course I knew how you felt about me—I would have been blind not to see it, dead not to sense it. But I never took advantage of your feelings to influence you. I was too honest for that—maybe foolishly honest. I wanted to keep you in school for the *right* reasons."

She was so articulate she threw him off balance—he couldn't argue with her because she overpowered him. Karl made a helpless gesture with his hands. "Why can't you believe that what I'm doing might be right for me?" he pleaded.

He was dismayed to see her eyes shimmer with tears. "I guess because I'm too proud . . . to admit that I've failed with a pupil who has as much personal worth as you have."

Karl went quickly to kneel beside her, resting his hand on her sleeve. "Oh no, you haven't failed," he said. "You taught me a lot of things I'd never have cared one bit about if it weren't for you."

"What sort of things?" she asked, sounding as if she really might cry.

"I can think of one of them right off." Karl patted her arm awkwardly before he got to his feet. "Stay right there. I'll show you."

He crossed the room to the piano and, standing, stroked a soft chord on the keyboard. As he began to sing the Shakespearean sonnet, he realized that she *had* taught him to understand how truthfully words could convey emotions. His voice wavered when he reached the quatrain:

> Nor dare I question with my jealous thought
> Where you may be, or your affairs suppose,
> But, like a sad slave, stay and think of nought
> Save, where you are, how happy you make those!

Karl envied them, the people she'd make happy—Charles Bonner and all her students in Canaan High School, the ones who would stay with her because it was right for them.

"That was lovely," Yulyona whispered when Karl had finished the sonnet. She came to him, her cheeks wet with tears. "I don't imagine we'll see much of each other from now on. I wish you well, Karl, I really do. If you ever need help in reaching your objectives, I hope you'll come to my husband and me."

"Thank you," he said. Silently he told her, I love you. Goodbye, Yulyona.

At the door of the mansion, Mary Margaret helped him into his coat. "Here's your hat," she said, handing it to him. "It's certainly good-looking. It's . . . appropriate for you." Her new poise was not yet entirely dependable—she blushed like the old Mary Margaret.

When she opened the door, Karl managed to smile for her. Then he started down the driveway, settling the homburg firmly on his head as he took a deep breath of the smoke-filled air.

AFTERWORD

"From the moment of his birth he'd heard the throb of the mills. It was as much a part of him as the sound of his heart beating beneath his skin." Based on accounts of work from the author's father, Karl Kerner's story is like many others from the mills of the "steel valley," reflecting a strong will to work and love of family and community. Karl, his family, and friends provide a vivid, intense picture of life in the mill towns of the Monongahela Valley in the time before World War I.

Born and raised in Duquesne, Pennsylvania—the town on which the Canaan of this novel is modeled—author Gloria Skurzynski was unaware of many of the ill effects of growing up in a mill town. In fact, she recalls that as a child, she "grew used to soot and smoky skies and the never-ending noise of the steel mill, and . . . actually rather liked it." Although the mills have been razed, people reminisce about the families who shared hard work, sorrow, and laughter; some say that echoes of those times can still be heard—or at least remembered.

Events that Skurzynski brings to life in *The Tempering* are sometimes funny, but also reveal the burden of grueling hours, low pay, and little concern for the workers' health or the environment. In spite of hardship and long hours, however, friendships were formed that lasted a lifetime. Those trials forged strong bonds within the community, uniting people from various ethnic and cultural backgrounds who might otherwise be enemies.

Though much of the physical evidence of western Pennsylvania's past has disappeared, *The Tempering* provides a window into the region's history. For those who would like to open more windows onto the rich themes explored by this book, please visit the Web site for *The Tempering* at http://www.pitt.edu/~press/goldentrianglebooks.

MARGARET MARY KIMMEL